THE
THAT
SIGHED

CLAUD
REGNARD

WILLOW OAK

ISBN 978-1-9160919-0-0

First printed edition 2019

Illustrations for *Summer Soufflé, Even an Old Sun Is Warm,* and *On the Dot* by Nantia Koulidou.

Illustrations for *The Last Train, Borrowed Time* and *The Books That ...* by Claud Regnard

Book cover photo and design by Claud Regnard

Printed in the UK by Beamreach Printing, 22 Pepper Street, Lymm, Cheshire, WA13 0JB. www.beamreachuk.co.uk

All gross proceeds from this edition go to help the work of St. Oswald's Hospice, Regent Avenue, Newcastle upon Tyne, NE3 1EE
and Wirral Hospice St. John's, Mount Road, Clatterbridge, Wirral, CH63 6JE

Published by WillowOak (logo © 2019 Reg no. 284 728 553)
WillowOakPiper@btinternet.com

About the author
Claud Regnard

Born in London of French parents, his first career ambition, aged five, was to be an astronaut. Two years later he changed his mind and decided to be a doctor. Despite that sensible choice and studying medicine in Scotland his subsequent career decisions were questionable. His first choice of surgery was based solely on his ability to rebuild the engine and gearbox on a Morris 1100. It was not his best career choice. Whilst training in general practice he came across a hospice but was advised that there was little to learn from such places. Consequently, four decades working in hospices and hospitals as a palliative care medicine consultant came as something of a surprise.

Now clinically retired he is proud to be an honorary consultant at St. Oswald's Hospice and to teach at Wirral Hospice St. John's, while maintaining interests in clinical decision making, implementing capacity legislation into clinical practice and identifying distress in individuals with severe communication difficulties. In between these interests and babysitting grandchildren he decided to translate some thoughts into short stories, some based on his experiences in hospice.

He continues to learn, which means that either there is a great deal more to life, hospice and palliative care than his advisors thought, or that Claud Regnard is a very slow learner.

CONTENTS

THE LAST TRAIN

She was alone on a cold bench in an empty station smothered in languid fog. In the silent, deep damp, even the clock had stopped, its soothing clockwork tick replaced by a steady drip of smoky water condensing from the iron roof beams. The fog swirled around the single light, condensing into a myriad of fine droplets before hurrying off into the shadows. No name or surroundings were visible in the grey murk and she could not remember how she had got here.

She could remember the foggy autumn days in wartime London when policemen would carry flaming torches in front of buses, the smoke thickening the smog. Unlike others, she found the gloom exciting, a muffled blanket that hid thoughts and actions and made the ordinary mysterious. The shadowy person on the corner could be a spy, a special operative or someone waiting to meet a secret partner. Perhaps she had always found the unusual exciting. When she was sixteen a flying circus had arrived near her village. She had gone with her father who had been fascinated by flying. Her uncle had encouraged them both, having often regaled them with his adventures on reconnaissance flights in the Great War. On arrival there was a small crowd. They paid their entrance fee and walked onto a grass field. The crowd murmurings increased as a distant speck became a noisy set of wings that swung low over the crowd, turned sharply and reappeared over their heads with sudden noise and smoke. Everyone was thrilled and they ran over to meet the pilot.

Captain Percival Phillips jumped out of his biplane, straight into Emily's heart.

'Welcome to the thrills of flying. Dare to fly and show your courage in the sky! Nowhere else can you feel as free while facing your own mortality with a smile. Fly above the earth and birds and discover the world above the clouds.'

Emily thought he was wonderful but her father thought he had the gift of the gab and was not keen on the way he was looking at Emily.

'My sturdy Avro defies gravity, races the wind and chases the stars. Now which of you has the gumption, the backbone, the sheer audacity to join me up there?'

Emily threw her hand up in the air.

'Well, there is a young lady with the right spirit! Off we go.'

Emily's father held on to her arm, but he knew that look of determination and let go, envious of her courage.

The captain helped her into the seat, secured her straps and fitted her with a leather flying helmet and goggles. He got into the seat behind her and gave his departure talk:

'I'm going to start the engine, taxi and take off. We'll do a few turns of the area. How brave are you feeling?'

'How good do you think you are?' replied Emily, with more cheek than courage.

'Ho, ho! Well spoken, young lady. Let's go!'

With a roar they were bouncing along the grass and she was suddenly pushed up into the air. It was glorious and frightening at the same time. He banked and she saw her father, uncle and the crowd like waiting ants. He turned again and her village appeared, a living map of home. The fields stretched to the horizon, a river drawing its silver thread across the woods and ploughed ground. An arrow of geese was drifting below her, calling out their surprise at the interloper. The captain rose towards the clouds. Suddenly everything was grey and she lost any sense of direction, floating alone with the moist air pushing against her face in a muffled, beguiling peace, unsure if she would ever see the world again. She turned to look behind her with wide, misty eyes.

'Come on young lady, snap to it! Time to go home.'

Emily opened her eyes. The greyness swirled around the cold station platform but her eyes partnered a smile at a past memory.

Unlike many others, her uncle had made wise investments after the Great War and was able to indulge in luxuries. She learnt to drive his Wolsey Hornet and an ageing R32 BMW motorbike, tearing around his farm and returning with her legs and back splattered like a modernist mud-mural. After a meeting with his accountant her uncle explained that he had a surprise for her and her father. They turned up at his barn as instructed. As they arrived his head popped around one door.

He opened the doors wide. 'I thought you might both be interested in this.'

Inside was an Avro 504K biplane.

'Anyone fancy a trip?'

Emily's uncle had learnt that keeping the plane in a barn generated a tax break as it could be classified as farm equipment. It meant Emily could learn to fly. Her father had misgivings but she soon wore him down with persistence. By the time the Second World War started, she had a pilot's licence and had been flying for over five years, often collecting feed, delivering farm products or just taking pleasure in flight. Joining the Women's Auxiliary Air Force and maintaining aircraft at RAF East Kirkby in Lincolnshire, did nothing to quench her fascination with flying. She was often reprimanded for staring at planes taking off and landing. Her fellow maintenance crew called her 'Airy Fairy Emily', mainly because they disbelieved her insistence that she could fly. Her chance to prove them wrong arrived when the Air Transport Auxiliary (ATA) finally allowed women to join. It had been established to recruit civilian pilots who could not join the RAF. They needed them to deliver planes from factories to airfields, freeing up pilots for the front line. Because of their age or handicaps the pilots in the ATA were known as 'Ancient and Tattered Airmen'. Once women could join, they were determined to be neither ancient nor tattered and earn the title they were later given, 'Attagirls'.

In 1942 Emily arrived at Haddenham Airfield near Oxford. Each day she and other ATA women would travel by bus to Barton-le-Clay in Bedfordshire for flying training, returning to Haddenham for lectures and learning mnemonics such as 'Hot Tempered MP Fancies Girls' which stood for Hydraulics, Trim, Tension, Mixture, Pitch, Petrol, Flaps, Gills and Gauges. Because of her previous flying experience Emily quickly progressed from the simple two-seater Miles Magsiter to the more complicated Fairey Swordfish. Each step was a thrill, mastering faster and more agile planes. When she completed her cross-country flights and conversion to the modern US-made Harvard trainer, it did not take long for her to get her Class II licence for fast single-engine fighters. Her first flight in the Spitfire Mk5 took her breath away. It had a sleek eager look, itching to leap into the sky. Flying it reminded her of that first flight with Captain Phillips, but with a push in her seat that felt like she was being launched into space. The power was thrilling, but mistakes were easy to make and she had her share of frights. Her instructor used to tell her 'That was a graveyard approach. Let's see if we can avoid the grave, shall we?'

She began to understand why the pioneer of female ATA pilots, Pauline Gower, sometimes called them 'Always Terrified Airwomen'.

On the platform, Emily thought she could hear a train whistle in the distance, but it was swallowed by the silence. It should have been cold in that swirling haze, but she felt oddly numb and shivered from the lack of feeling. It had been like that after Robert died. On a foggy London street, outside the Lyons Corner House in the Strand, they had literally bumped into each other in the opaque air. As an apology Robert had offered Emily tea. He was a dashing young fighter pilot with the standard handle-bar moustache, and she was a forthright woman whose dark flowing hair hid a gentle smile. Having fallen for flying they were now falling for each other. That week of leave was a round of dances, walks in misty London and snuggling in the cinema. The nights together included one on a London Underground platform during an air raid with no prospect of intimacy. She suspected that her father would have considered it very suitable for a young unmarried woman.

Emily and Robert exchanged goodbyes the next day, each determined to meet again. When she did not hear from him she wondered if their time had just been a wartime fling. She decided to face Robert, if only to give him a piece of her mind. It was another foggy evening at his airfield and in the mess she saw a friend of his they had met in London. He had been laughing and drinking until he saw her. His pale face was the warning she had dreaded. Outside, in that dark fog, she learnt that Robert had been shot down over the Channel two days earlier. The plane had exploded and there was no chance he would still be alive. She hugged the tear-streaked face in front of her and ran to the bus. On the way home, her tears were hidden by the condensed rivulets trickling down the window. Her return to work was accompanied by a cold steel that numbed her heart.

Within days she picked up a new Supermarine Spitfire for delivery to Hartford Bridge near RAF Farnborough. ATA pilots navigated using maps, a compass and a watch to estimate how far they had travelled. There were usually enough rivers, roads and railway lines to indicate the route. They were taught that clouds meant death, but Emily found them more fun than dangerous. Leaving on a dull day and climbing through the grey into bright sunshine was a joy, watching the soft pillows float by below. Even more magical was entering into clear air between two cloud layers with the sensation of speed matched above and below. Heavy cloud was a nuisance and it was easy to get disorientated, but it was usually possible to drop low enough into clearer air. Even fog could not obscure taller buildings or hills. The danger was a combination.

It was a cold sunny day taking off from Hamble with reasonable weather predicted around Oxford. But within 10 minutes she was in thick cloud. Climbing above the cloud was strongly discouraged as there was no certainty pilots would find a gap to see land. Dropping as low as she dared to find clear air revealed nothing but grey. More than half way with no certainty of finding her way back to Hamble, she climbed to 1100 feet to be sure of clearing the North Wessex Downs. The only choice was to use the compass for direction and the horizontal indicator to make sure she was not plummeting to earth or climbing to a stall. But the grey was beginning to press in on her, followed by that familiar, gentle sensation of floating. Perhaps this was how she was going to meet her beloved Robert, when the voice of Captain Phillips on her first flight shouted, 'Come on young lady, snap to it!'

Realising she was fast losing altitude she pulled up and focused on her watch. A quick calculation told her she should be over the airfield at Hartford Bridge, but there was nothing below. Certain that she was close she started a series of turns, hoping to see something. Each turn was confusing, pushing her into the seat but scrambling any feeling of which way was up. Using the horizontal indicator to keep her safe she kept trying to see anything in the murk below. Perhaps this was not just going to be a graveyard approach but landing in the grave itself.

Suddenly on her fifth turn she smelt burning fuel. Sure she was on fire she checked her instrument panel but everything was normal. Then in the mirror she saw a sheet of flame shoot up behind her. Turning again, she could see two parallel lines of flame on the ground, running rapidly into the distance. They had lit some sort of beacon. Flying parallel to the lines she turned to head directly back between the burning markers. As she descended she could see the runway and was suddenly in a tunnel of clear air.

Back in the mess she was met by the squadron leader at Hartford Bridge.

'I see you've met Fido,' he said with a smile.

Emily looked around for a four-legged friend.

'Ha! No, FIDO – Fog Intense Dispersal Operation. Damn handy thing too. We heard some idiot circling above us trying to land and lit the fuel pipes. The heat lifts the fog up to 300 feet. Turns out the idiot was you and a damn pretty and brave one too, I must say!'

Normally Emily would have bristled at the pretty comment but she could not help feeling that Robert would have been proud to hear her being called brave.

It seemed impossible that a fog could get any thicker and yet this one began to creep over the platform edge like a snake on the prowl. She missed her blue Ferry Pilots book. That told you what to do. At least it told you how to fly dozens of different aircraft types. The handling notes made clear which controls did what, with advice on what you could do and must never do. On occasions the notes were the only instruction she had about a plane. As Emily's experience grew she progressed to a Class V licence which allowed her to fly bombers. Compared to the Spitfire they were lumbering giants, but the sound of several mighty engines at full throttle was a thrill. She had been tasked with delivering a bomber to the same airfield where she had once worked in the maintenance crews. Making sure the weather was good all the way, she took off and landed without problems. As she came to a stop she gathered her belongings, made sure she looked presentable, opened the exit hatch and climbed down the ladder. All the ground crew could see was a pair of leather boots appear and descend the ladder. She took off her helmet and brushed her long hair away from her face. The eyes of the ground crew remained on the doorway.

'Are you waiting for someone, lads?' asked Emily sweetly.

'The pilot, Miss, he shouldn't be long.'

'I'm afraid you are under a misapprehension boys. Only one pilot on duty today.'

They stopped as realisation dawned.

Emily's smile grew wider with the satisfaction of knowing that 'Airy Fairy' Emily was in the past. 'Come on, which of you lovely boys is going to buy me a beer?'

Not even the fog could slow the progress of Emily's laughter as it echoed along the station roof. She remembered the laughter with Robert, her nephews and nieces, the pupils at the aero club she set up after the war, her friends and colleagues. She lived long enough to see television, computers, Star Wars and mobile phones. Even in the hospice she remembered laughing at the memories she shared with family and nurses, but few events had given her as much pleasure as stepping off that bomber.

As the laughter faded she heard a train clank and screech its way slowly into the station. A large black shape hissed and spat, its cab glowing orange from the burning coals. The carriages eased gently to a halt. They were light, warm and welcoming. Some people were making their way onto the train. She had not noticed them before, hidden by the fog. Emily got up and opened one of the doors, to see others sitting there silently, some smiling at her. It was too much. She stepped back onto the platform into the numb, floating but familiar greyness. Thinking she might stay there for a while longer, she was roused by remembered voices:

'Anyone fancy a trip?'

'Young lady, snap to it! Time to go home.'

Then she noticed someone gripping her elbow and felt her father let go all those years ago.

She climbed into the carriage and sat in the comfortable seat. Almost immediately the train started to move and at the same time the second hand on the station clock begun its journey around the numbers. She was going to see Robert at last.

For additional information on The Last Train
see p267

SUMMER SOUFFLÉ

The beach huts sat hunched in the glare, pastel soldiers resolute in their resistance to the heat. Any weeds were gently browning under the sun or pockmarked with white weed killer. Only suitable plants were allowed. Sam knew how they felt.

He sauntered past the bleached boxes like a lost sand grain drifting in a lazy breeze. He was in no hurry, keeping to the shadows, partly to keep cool but mainly to stay hidden. Not that many noticed a thin, bedraggled dog. A few children spotted him. Some pointed him out to adults, some were curious, a few threw whatever was to hand – sand, a sandwich or seashell. But by the time the adults looked, the child stared or an object landed he was far way, leaving the viewer uncertain if they had seen anything at all.

His memory of being little was the warm, milky comfort of his mum. That memory was brief but intense. Some smells flashed him back to snuggling against her fur. That feeling of warm peace would last him much of the day until the need for food became a priority. But once he had eaten and found somewhere safe he would snooze and dream more memories.

He remembered being taken to the house of a retired farmer who once owned collies to herd the sheep. The farmer had always kept the dogs outside, whatever the season. Sam could see a red balloon of a face looking at him sternly and being taken to a cold kennel in his back garden. All Sam could do was howl for his mum, warmth and company. Most evenings neighbours at the bottom of the garden would call to him and he would sniff their hands shyly. He heard the neighbours' voices speaking to the farmer's wife and soon after the farmer's wife brought Sam a cloth to sleep against. It helped a little but did not stop Sam's howls of loneliness, until he felt himself lifted inside by the farmer's wife. There he sat by the fire, where her large hands warmed his small heart. In time the farmer's face thawed to a smile and he allowed Sam to doze at his feet, curled against his woolly slippers.

Christmas passed chasing the tinsel and wrapping paper. It drifted into a New Year of cold fluff from the sky. Sam remembered his first walk through snow, starting with anxious creaking steps followed by thrilling dives into comforting, cold silence. Any chill was matched by warm excitement, followed by the heat of the fire.

Those safe days slipped by too quickly. There came a time when the farmer took to his bed but Sam still curled against the now empty slippers. The farmer's wife would sleep in a chair by the bed, occasionally reaching down to stroke Sam. Looking up, Sam saw her smile was warm but her eyes were distant. When a crowd of new feet walked in accompanied by whispering and crying, Sam hid under the bed. The slippers disappeared from the house along with any warmth and kindness. After that he remembered only cold and fear.

The farmer's wife became too unwell to look after Sam and he was taken by a relative. Once again he was in an outside kennel, but this time in a concrete yard. Winter still had its time to run and he experienced cold, hunger and beatings. There was no pattern to the punishments, no way to avoid them, especially when the man staggered in late at night with a bad smell about him. His face was always screwed up like the wrapping paper Sam used to chase, but with no warmth or colour. His hands were cold like his food, and his clothes smelt of decay. Sam had found an old slipper in the yard, definitely not the farmer's, but it helped him remember better times. One evening the man was in an angry mood and reached in, found the slipper and pulled it out. Sam bit down hard on the slipper, growling. The man yelled as Sam's teeth sank into his hand. The beating that evening made it hard for Sam to breathe or see through his swollen eye. In the morning, Sam found himself tied to the kennel by a rope that squeezed his neck when he pulled.

That cold, dank morning Sam wondered if he should rest, stop fighting and let go. It would be so easy. He would see his mum again and the kind balloon face of the farmer. But he had changed. There was anger in young Sam that refused to be subdued. He had noticed the man had begun to leave through the back gate to empty rubbish that smelt little different to the man. He had seen that his rope, like the man, was tired and rotten. Chewing through the rope gave him a purpose and eased his hunger for a while. He waited.

One dark evening, an exhausted sleep was interrupted by a clatter as the rubbish-smelling man came out carrying a large bag. The man staggered to the gate, rattled the latch open and stepped through. Sam crept silently out of the kennel and ran through the man's legs. He could hear the man swearing, shouting and then falling, hitting something on the way down. Sam's chest ached with bruised, weak muscles but he kept going. He never looked back. He hid in corners, taking food where he could, but finding little comfort. He learnt to keep away from people. In turn they kept away from him, unsure what he might do or spread.

Jack preferred to shrink into the shade. The shadows hid his gaze, just like those passing hid theirs. The alcoves provided shelter from the weather but not from insults, so the dark provided an escape. He could not escape the memories that followed him into the darkest places but sometimes shone a little light and warmth on his soul. As a child he had lived happily enough on his parents' farm. He worked hard, helping his father, crunching his way through dark morning frozen grass to collect the cows for milking or to help deliver lambs. It fascinated him to see those floppy wet bundles of legs wriggle into life, wobble upright and hungrily suck up their first milk. Occasionally a lamb was rejected and Jack was given the task of feeding bottled milk to a hungry mouth on gangly woolly stilts. Afterwards it would stare at Jack's eyes and fall asleep like a child in a tightly knitted jumper. Those eyes did not question or judge. He missed that accepting face.

But those rare moments of solitude with sleepy lambs became distant memories. Too often he was met with accusations of laziness and lectures on honest work in the fields. To Jack the honest truth was that his life had become mind numbing and bone chilling. His hatred for the cold and the dark blinded him to the end of winter. As the days lengthened, he resented wasting the light on mud and cows. He no longer saw acceptance in the lambs, but indifference. He had become a stranger to them and to himself. His mother sensed the change and it frightened her. His father just became angry. He saw the farm as a living creature that needed care, but Jack saw it as a monster that was draining their lives. The arguments became raw and painful. The last time Jack saw his parents his mother was crying and his red-faced father was shouting at him to get out.

He spent the next few weeks walking, sleeping in fields, catching lifts and finding food where he could. Usually this was from bins outside cafes. Being chased away by angry cooks became a game that affirmed his freedom. At other times trouble followed Jack like a delinquent twin, resulting in drunken fights. Like his life, he had no idea where he was going but kept heading halfway between the rising and setting sun. Before long the land stopped and he was facing a sea, lazing in a reddening sun. It brought warmth to his liberty but no escape from hunger and tiredness.

Jack walked down an embankment to an old abandoned railway station. Crunching over the broken glass of the waiting room he found a trap door that took him to a store room below. Here the day's sun had warmed the old bricks and protected him from a chilly sea breeze. The remaining rays of a rusty sun crept through an opening next to the railway track. He lay down amid the warm dust and dreamed of the times he had been to the seaside as a child on rare holidays with a neighbour's family. There had been a wonder in seeing the water glittering through screwed up eyes and intense pleasure at the ice cream strawberry sweetness slipping down his throat. Sleepy memories were a welcome salve for the soul that night.

Down by the beach huts, sizzled parents and frazzled children were gathering their sand-salted belongings.

Sam watched from the shadows as a child was given an ice cream bribe. The odds of getting some slippery pink bliss were looking up. On cue, the child dropped his ice cream. While the crying child and arguing parents walked off, Sam's straggle of fur shot out of the shadows, grasped the cone in his jaws and disappeared, leaving a trail of pale pink drops. Sam adored ice cream. It was worth being seen by humans just to taste that icy smooth, sweet liquid. Not that anyone ever followed him. Who would want a melting blob that had been scraped off the floor by a slobbering mouth? And yet something was chasing him now. He raced into the shadows behind the bins, but the shape followed. He pushed past the bins into the narrow dark between the beach huts, but the clutter of the bins was followed by scattering sounds nearby. Whatever was following him was no longer interested in ice cream which was now pink rivulets down his front legs. He froze. Near him something was starting to snuffle and growl.

Sam had had his share of meetings with fellow dogs. Some kept to themselves, some were unpleasantly friendly, some were desperate, but a few just hated everyone and everything. The sound and smell nearby was hate, hate that would finish him off faster than he could devour his ice cream. Sam dropped the melting mess and turned his head to look for a way out. The gap between two huts was blocked by a fallen plank, but this was angled up to the beach hut roofs. Slowly Sam started to climb the smooth wood. As he reached the top he could smell the sun-heated bitumen and free air. It was then that he slipped.

His nails dug into the wood and made a sound that echoed between the huts. The snuffling stopped, but the growling got deeper. Sam scrabbled the last inches onto the hut roof to meet a volley of angry barking. A set of dirty teeth jumped up and he stared into a pair of bloodshot eyes. Fortunately the huts were too high for those teeth to get close. The only option was to run. Hut occupants ran out to see one dog scrambling across the roofs, with brief flashes of another leaping up the back walls like a demented kangaroo. In the distance Sam could see the last beach hut getting close. He was just ahead of the teeth and eyes. Beyond was the flat roof of the beach cafe. From the apex of the last beach hut Sam leapt onto the flat roof and then onto the railway embankment. The angry sounds receded behind him.

Sam was exhausted. His anger at the wasted ice cream was tempered by the relief of escape. He sauntered slowly along the railway line, through the hazy tar smells of the sleepers. It was dusk now and the cooling rails swept around a corner in the cliffs. He was just thinking about finding a nook for the night when he heard a growl back down the track. Looking back was a familiar large shape with growling teeth. Sam started to run. Behind him the large dog clattered stones against the rails with a clanging echo along the metal. The ringing was getting closer and he could hear the rasping breaths. He was no longer sure if he was imagining the breath-stink or if it was just behind him. As the track curved ahead a platform came into view. His paws were being cut by the sharp stones and he had little breath left. Stopping meant death. The platform had no shelter, but next to the track was a dark opening. Sam leapt through.

Jack was jerked awake by angry barking and then hit by a bundle of fur that smelt of strawberry. He had no time to wonder about the smell as an angry head started to come through the opening. The head hesitated, unsure of the darkness and the unfamiliar smell. A large paw appeared and even in the dimming light Jack could see the bared teeth. Jack reached out and felt a half brick. A hollow echo bounced in the darkness as the brick hit the wall next to the opening. The growling head hesitated, puzzled by the direction of the threat. But the growl started again and the head pushed further in. Jack picked up any rubble he could. It was mainly small stones and dust but this time he threw it at the head and kept picking and throwing. The eyes blinked with dust and the head jerked as each small stone hit. The final insult was the large paw being bitten by sharp teeth. The head pulled out whimpering and ran back down the track, still puzzled why shadows that smelt of strawberry ice cream could be so dangerous.

It was dark now, with only a little moonlight creeping through the opening. Jack heard whimpering and could just make out an unfamiliar shape. Sam lay trembling in the corner. All his life Sam had known what was coming next, good or bad. For the first time he was unsure. He heard a rustle of paper followed by something landing near his nose. The thought that this was a bad aim was dispelled by the smell of meat and bread. Sam ate in gulps with greed, then pleasure. He lay down, licking the last remains and looked at his companion. He was difficult to make out, but Sam was surprised by the smile. In the shadow a hand reached out. Not the bad smell of the rubbish man but one of the streets and earth. Just like Sam. Exhaustion allowed the hand to touch him and gently stroke behind his ear. Sam tilted his head with pleasure. The strokes became less and were soon replaced by Jack's snoring, but the hand remained, warm and safe. Before long Sam joined in the snoring chorus.

As the early dawn painted watercolours on the wall, two pairs of eyes opened and glared at each other. Memories of fearful escapes were slowly replaced by a shared relief that they had survived this far. Trust would take longer. It was safer to share wariness.

The first day was spent together but at a safe distance. They showed each other where they found food and hiding places. Jack's food was often cold greasy burgers that gave Sam's teeth an unpleasantly sticky coating. Sam's food choice was bone scraps that made Jack want to throw up. Sam's hiding places barely fitted Sam, let alone Jack with three layers of clothes. Jack's places of safety were too exposed for Sam unless he hid behind Jack. Neither was impressed by the other's choices. At the end of that first day, they each began to doubt this partnership would work.

It had started to rain heavily and they took shelter in a doorway. People hurried by, gliding under umbrellas, as if a single drop of rain would ruin their lives. As the rain eased, however, Jack noticed people staring at him. He was not used to attention, but what he could not see was Sam behind him, peeking out at the dwindling rain.

Over the years Sam had cultivated a lost puppy look that sometimes brought dividends of food. On this occasion Sam wasn't even aware he was looking pathetic, but a few people noticed him and smiled. Before long a small coin fell into Jack's lap, followed by an offer of coffee and a sandwich. Jack had avoided begging. He had seen too many sink into a cycle of alcohol, drugs, cold and death. He had visited shelters on occasions but found them full of a sadness that eclipsed the kindness of those helping. However, begging with a small dog brought dividends of food and some money, even dog food. One couple walked past and the woman turned back, reaching into her handbag and silently handed Jack a £20 note. That would buy food for both of them. As they returned to the derelict station, Sam and Jack began to think there might be a benefit to this partnership after all.

Autumn had started to spread its misty softness, lit with occasional scarlet leaves drifting along a damp earth. Each sunset the beach huts were embarrassed by the brightly coloured leaves piled against them, as if being taunted that their time was ending. Some days a retreating sun brought a reminder of warmth, but the evenings drew in earlier and colder to make clear who was winning the race. Leaves would drift under the station platform, blown cold as a winter warning. Few people ventured out except those who thought cold air and exercise could delay old age. They were too obsessed with their losing battle to worry about a bundle of clothes and fur in a doorway.

Jack and Sam went back to searching bins, despite having to prise them open on frosty mornings. Cold grease and bone bits were some comfort over the cold. Kitchen staff were less likely to chase Jack if they had snarling teeth at their backsides and Sam was too quick to be caught. One evening they were searching bins behind a care home. The kitchen door slammed open, and with the light streamed out three angry-looking cooks. Jack turned to run while Sam prepared to find the nearest backside when the three cooks pushed Jack aside and ran off. Looking back at the kitchen the light was flickering with dark smoke as the fire took hold.

Jack and Sam went to the front as staff evacuated residents to the raucous accompaniment of fire alarms. In the distance he could hear sirens. Sam barked and looked up. Following his gaze Jack saw an open window and a face shouting. Everyone was busy helping and no-one had noticed. Jack told Sam to stay and ran into the house. The fire was taking hold in the kitchen and smoke was creeping rapidly along the ceiling of the hall. He ran up the stairs to be faced with a dozen doors. Disorientated, he was unsure which to try when he felt a tug on his trousers. Sam had ignored his order and was pulling him to one door. In the room a woman was in a wheelchair at the window. She had covered her head with a blanket to avoid the smoke, but as Jack wheeled her out to the top of the stairs the smoke was rapidly getting closer to the ground. The only option was to bounce the wheelchair down, step by step. The smoke followed them down the steps. At the bottom Jack and the woman were coughing with the smoke and Jack was dizzy and blind with tears. The front door was shrouded in smoke but Sam was below the smoke and pushed Jack from behind, towards the front door and clean air.

Outside, the woman was taken away by the firemen. Jack sat down on the steps as the fire was brought under control. Sam had followed the wheelchair and watched them give the woman a mask to breathe. Her hand dropped and found Sam. He looked up at a soot-covered face and a pair of smiling eyes that brought back memories of warmth and love. Jack saw the woman being lifted into the ambulance and saw recognition in her face.

Sam and Jack slipped silently back to their station sanctuary. The next morning they had a visit to make, but that night Sam and Jack slept side by side, dreaming of sleepy beach huts, cool ice cream and summer smiles.

For additional information on Summer Soufflé
see p268

Summer Soufflé

Sea sated smiles,
Silly sunhats,
Sagging seats

Sunny sautéed scenes
Salty scents,
Simmering sands

Suntanned swimmers,
Scarlet skin,
Screaming shorts

Sleepy sails
Slowly sliding,
Scarcely sailing

Soggy salmon sandwich,
Sandy sausage,
Sweet sun oil

Seeping shabbiness
Shimmying shadows
Sharing shelter

Scooped sandcastles,
Scrunched sculptures,
Scuttling shells

Scarcely serious
Summer soufflé

EVEN AN OLD SUN IS WARM

George and Ethel were rosy, round and a ripe old age. They were both short of money, hair and a good pair of knees, but this never stopped them going on holiday. It also never stopped Ethel telling George what and how to pack, and only his good nature stopped him emptying the suitcase over her head. When the weatherman forecast a heatwave George had thought of Blackpool, but Ethel wanted a real journey, to Scotland this time. After 56 years together it was hardly expecting too much. It was expecting a lot of their old car, which had creaked its way north, the occupants steaming with the heat as much as the engine. Eventually an overheated engine had called a halt; George knew exactly how the engine felt.

They arrived on the shores of Loch Shiel early in the afternoon. The small hotel opposite the water was affordable and peaceful, surrounded by hills of heather, ferns and rocks ground down by time. A peaty stream tumbled through the rocks nearby, happily skipping its way to the loch. Just visible up the loch was the Green Isle, a small grassy mound topped by a ruined chapel. The landlady explained that it was dedicated to St. Finan, a holy man in old times. The isle had been a site of pilgrimage, and on the hillsides you could still see the stones marking the paths to the isle, looking like lonely soldiers marching to long-lost villages. The loch cooled George and Ethel's tempers and the good tea ensured they were not about to lose their rounded shapes. George admitted this place was quieter than Blackpool, but he still missed the beach. Practical as usual, Ethel had a solution. There was a beach nearby and although it was early evening, Midsummer's day in the north-west Highlands ensured good light for many hours.

They arrived on an empty beach. The distant islands floated above the haze and the white shell sands reflected the turquoise of the sea. The heat on the ancient rocks seemed to make the air heavy and slow. George and Ethel soaked up the sun like a pair of lazy leatherback turtles. Ethel lay face down on the sand, busily rearranging the sand as she snored. George sat back, gazing lazily at the quiet waves. Through the haze, he vaguely noticed the occasional bird drifting its way home across the water. One bird seemed in a hurry and he imagined it getting a mouthful for staying out too late with the lads at the local cliff. It must have been feeling very guilty tonight because it seemed to be travelling faster and faster. It was when it instantly changed direction towards them and accelerated that George focused.

'Look at THAT!' George shouted.

Ethel snorted a bit of the beach up her left nostril, rolled upright and spluttered a mixture of sand and abuse. She was silenced by the look on George's face and looked to where he was pointing. Low across the water something was coming at them very fast.

The silence held their breaths as the shape flashed overhead, their upturned faces reflected on a mirror underside. Their wide eyes met, just as a wall of sea spray hit them and the sand around was blown into the air. Ethel helped George to his feet just in time to see the small speck vanishing over the hill towards Loch Shiel.

Ethel was already striding back to the car. 'Come on, let's follow it!'

George wasn't so sure. Things like this didn't happen in Blackpool. Trams or buses didn't sneak up – you knew where they were going, and if you missed one, three would be along later. They also approached at a sensible speed. The only things in the air now were robber seagulls and one fluorescent kite attached to a small child. But George could predict one thing: stay behind and Ethel would make this holiday miserable. With his mind screaming 'Stay!' his body calmly got in the car and they drove back to the loch.

The loch was as peaceful as when they had left. George parked the car and they walked to the hotel. The landlady was leaning on her gate, looking at the loch. Ethel could hardly contain herself.

'Did you see anything fly up the loch?'

The landlady kept staring at the loch. 'Och, we've jets on exercise around here, things flying so low they frighten the lambs with the noise.'

'But what we saw was silent. Strangest thing, nothing like a jet. It frightened me half to death.'

George noted that it had scared him more than half way and he wasn't sure when he would stop feeling scared.

'Well, I may have seen something go up the loch. Quiet it was, like you said. Probably one of them hanging-gliders. More wind than sense if you ask me.'

According to her story everything was cosy and normal, but she had a puzzled look, as if a local sheep had just said 'Hello!' and was now calmly chewing the grass the way it had always done. Ethel was getting excited. George could tell because her voice became precise and quiet, just like it did when she was trying to get him to admit he had broken something.

'And what did this "some-thing" look like?' Ethel enunciated slowly.

'Difficult to tell against the hill, but it seemed to slow as it got to the Isle.'

'Do - you - mean - it - landed - there?' Ethel's words were getting very precise.

'Yes, - it - did - seem - to - land - there. Didn't - you - see - it?' articulated the landlady, copying Ethel's way of speaking.

You could see Ethel was not used to someone using her method of getting information. She moved back slightly, coughed, and muttered a surprisingly quiet 'No'. George was impressed and reminded himself to try the landlady's technique.

'George, I want to go onto that island. Now.' Ethel had shifted into determined mode.

For a second, George had thought of trying out this new-found technique of communication, but decided that defying a determined Ethel was unwise. Anyway, he might want to practise it alone before trying it out for real.

'There's a small motor boat at the jetty,' the landlady explained, fully recovered. 'If you want, I'll ready it for you.'

'There's no need to go to all that trouble....,' started George.

The landlady looked at Ethel with a satisfied smile. 'No trouble at all.'

'Thank you,' Ethel threw back over her shoulder as she strode towards the jetty.

Whether George was still shocked from his earlier experience or whether he knew that life was simpler this way, he found himself on open water heading up the loch. It was easier than he had thought. In fact, here in the open air he was quite enjoying himself. He couldn't help quietly smiling at seeing a rather pale Ethel gripping the rail with white knuckles.

Within ten minutes they were close to the Green Isle. The sun was setting and the last rays caught the ruined chapel in its warm caress. They tied the boat to the small landing stage and walked up the grassy slope. The island was small and George reckoned it would only take ten minutes to walk around its edge. Dotted amongst the rocks and shrubs were tombstones, most of which were from the past 150 years, although a few were much older. George puzzled at the neatly cut grass and why someone should want to come all this way to mow the lawn, but a white shape amongst the rocks explained why. The local resident sheep was doing its efficient best, getting into all the corners a lawnmower could never reach.

The chapel lay on the top of the island, only its walls standing as testament to the past. An old bell was lying on the stone altar, daring anyone to pick it up and summon the ghosts. It should have been an eerie place, but the warm air and the light evening simply made it peaceful. They were almost back to where they had started and even Ethel seemed more at ease as she rounded the chapel wall.

That was when she saw them.

Ethel had been so sure she would find a spaceship with strange creatures. She had expected something extraordinary, but not this. Indeed, what was extraordinary was that they were so ordinary. After seeing the strangest event in your life you do not expect to meet another grey-haired couple walking towards you, he in cotton shorts and her in a floral print dress. Ethel's impulse was to ask her where she had got the dress, but any words stayed frozen in her brain. George now realised that Ethel's chase had been a bit of nonsense. He briskly walked up to the couple and introduced himself and Ethel. The man smiled, saying, 'Hallo, I am Joseph and this is Louise. Pleased to meet you.'

It was not often that George had seen Ethel lost for words. George, however, thought they seemed a nice couple and invited them back to the hotel for a drink. Ethel felt better on the way back, especially after two whiskies at the hotel. Soon Louise and Ethel were enjoying each other's company. George felt at ease with Joseph and they got busy arranging some short trips in the surrounding area.

On the beach the next morning, the events of the previous evening faded in the warm clear air; it was a time to relax and chat with friends. The next few days were spent in each other's company – new friends who felt they had known each other for years. Ethel and George felt a genuine sadness as a few days later the couples waved goodbye to each other. It was only as George drove away that he realised that when they had met Joseph and Louise on the island, he had not seen or heard any other boat and he had no idea how they had got onto the island.

The names Joseph and Louise seemed to fit well enough, at least Louise thought so. Louise was still counting how long they had been together, whilst Joseph was still pretending he knew. She had wanted a quieter holiday this time, away from the bustle of busy ports or leisure centres. Joseph liked such places, but this holiday seemed pleasant enough without stretching their money. They had needed some help learning the most commonly used language, but there had been so much time on the trip they had managed well enough. Renting transport had been difficult. The problem was finding an affordable runabout that could cope with a trip to the edge of the galaxy.

The journey had been pleasant, but meeting George and Ethel on the island had been a real surprise. Later in the hotel Ethel had talked excitedly about what they had seen and her disappointment at not finding a spaceship. Louise had smiled as she thought about the state of their transport – one of the power packs should have been replaced aeons ago, the cloaking device was stuck in 'rock' mode, and she dare not mention what the previous owners had been up to in the zero gravity chamber. Both it and they were past their best. Louise had no heart to tell Ethel that her aliens were just an old couple short on time and money, so Louise had left Ethel to her dreams. All four of them were getting older, but they still knew how to enjoy themselves.

Even an old sun is warm.

For additional information on Even an Old Sun is Warm, see p269

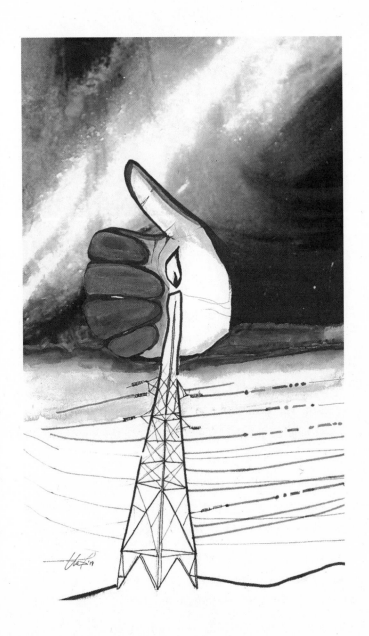

ON THE DOT

It was wet enough to drown the sun. Roger dripped off the bus, tightened his raincoat and got out his umbrella. He was pleased he had dubbined his boots as he sloshed his way towards the entrance of RAF Elvington. He leant his sturdy brolly into the slanting rain and headed for the control tower. In the small radio room below, Freddie and Alfie were huddled around three cups of hot chocolate. Together they sipped the sweet liquid in the vague hope it would warm their spirits. For a while they gazed with pride at the rows of vintage radio equipment they had restored. It had taken years to find all the parts, repair and rebuild each component. They remembered the first time they had powered up. Any satisfaction that nothing had fused or burnt out was nothing compared to the pride of getting a response to their first message. They had modern radio equipment there too, but it was the fading, flaking boxes they loved, with their valves smelling of ozone and dust.

Visitors would drift by, unsure if they were maintenance crew, a sad re-enactment event or elderly visitors sheltering from the weather. The few who came in were interested and listened to their tales of distant contacts. Some even noticed the Morse Code key on the desk, assuming it was a cosmetic addition to the ambiance. Most were surprised that it was still in regular use, but when one of the three tried explaining that it would be the only form of worldwide communication in the event of a solar storm, most visitors smiled weakly and left, suspecting the men's brain cells were as antique as their radios.

In reality, the men's neurons had assimilated and mulled over the facts. To the rare visitor intrigued by solar storms they were treated to a triple act. First Roger would reel off some facts:

'In 1770, nine days of red skies in Asia were thought to have been aurora caused by a huge solar storm.' He started to warm to the task, 'Then, in 1859 another storm caused aurora to be visible in Rome, bright enough to read at night and to cause telegraph operators to get electric *shocks*.' Roger liked to emphasise the last word to get the rare visitor's attention.

'One in 1940 damaged phone cables, while two storms in 2003 and 2005 disrupted satellites, power grids and global positioning systems. Did you know that solar storms are classed as B, C, M and X, each being ten times more powerful than the previous?'

The rare visitor would shake their head.

'The X category has an unlimited number of levels, each level indicating a strength ten times stronger than the one before. The storm in 2003 was a category X FORTY FIVE level,' he stated loudly, making sure the number had the necessary gravitas. 'In 2012 a solar storm developed that was the same severity as the one in 1859 but just missed the earth. That's a thought to keep you awake at night....'

By now any rare visitor was on the endangered species list. If they were still paying attention and, even better, nodding with interest, Alfie took over.

'Damage to electricity transformers is the biggest problem, as ordering, manufacturing and installing replacements can take 1 to 2 years. But that's not the worst.' He would pause here for effect.

'Any damage to satellite communications and global positioning systems will cause extensive disruption.'

If the visitor made the mistake of asking when this might happen, Freddie was ready, waiting: 'The next active cycle should peak in 2024 and be relatively weak. But a freak X9 storm in 2017 occurred during a supposed quiet period, and that suggests that predictions can be wildly out. It could happen tomorrow.'

At this point the visitor would either be looking anxious and suffer insomnia for several nights, or go into denial mode when their partner told them to stop being silly and find the toilets.

Roger, Freddie and Alfie had a healthy distrust of governments and large energy firms who claimed that early warning from satellites and electricity grid protection made the UK 'resilient'. Official reports were very fond of that word, using it like a spell to ward off evil. The three suspected that resilient meant 'absorbent' and they knew it was folks like them who would be doing the soaking up. They had plenty of experience during the Second World War of absorbing enemy attacks, and Roger's grandfather knew exactly what it meant to go over the top in the First World War and soak up enemy gunfire. No doubt the generals of both wars were equally fond of the word 'resilient'. In the cold radio room looking out on a soggy airfield, Roger, Freddie and Alfie were not feeling very resilient.

Preparation helped. Alfie and his young family had seen the Cuba missile crisis and gone through the fear of nuclear war. With his wife he had prepared for the worst, pulling together a trunk full of dried food ready to put in their car. They had worked out the best place to go – the north-west of Scotland was the least likely place to suffer from fallout. In their many trips to Gairloch and Ullapool they had even found a derelict Victorian hunting lodge that could be their temporary home. Whether they could have guessed when to evacuate with sufficient notice was a moot point, but they had felt they were doing something positive, the alternative being to pretend it would never happen. Denial had never seemed a reliable survival strategy, although it gave an excellent impression of resilience.

The fact that nuclear war never happened had not dented Alfie's survival instinct. He had long kept a store of food and wood, plus a 1960 BSA M21 motorcycle and sidecar that he had bought from the AA when they made the final switch to patrol cars in 1968. He had enjoyed restoring it to top condition. He kept a separate passenger side car and used to take his wife and daughter for short trips, in the days when health and safety were mere twinkles in an officious eye. Over the years he had made sure it was still running and securely locked in his garden shed.

At the airfield he insisted the antenna was disconnected and nothing was left switched on in the radio room. He had tried to line the walls with plastic sheets and aluminium foil to protect against a magnetic solar storm. Alfie's daughter Chloe had wondered why she always ran out of kitchen foil after he visited. Freddie and Roger understood Alfie's need to prepare for the worst, but even they thought the kitchen foil made the radio room look like a nursery school production of *Star Trek*. Alfie had to suspend his redecorating when he realised he needed to cover the floor and door. Freddie was adamant that enough was enough. He had no intention of spending his last moments in a tin can coffin, no matter how sparkly and shiny. As a compromise, Alfie found an old metal cabinet which was large enough to provide a useful electrical cage to protect any vulnerable equipment, but too small to fit Freddie inside.

Roger woke to the early morning sunlight drawing dappled shadows on his window blind. He was in no rush to get up and rolled over for a snooze, but a glance at his clock halted any thoughts of sleep. It was 3.30am, long before the sunrise. He opened the blind and stared in awe. Across the sky, ribbons of glowing beads meandered below drapes of light. The beads swelled until the sky was enveloped in shifting curtains of translucent waterfalls, changing from yellow to green, red, blue and then purple and violet. The last colours made Roger stumble back. He knew that they occurred at much lower altitudes and suggested a powerful solar storm. He tried to contact Freddie and Alfie on their mobiles but there was just static. At least the lights were still on as Roger got dressed, climbed into his car and drove to Freddie's house.

Freddie was standing at his front door, open mouthed. 'This is it, isn't it?'

Roger had his serious face on, 'Looks like it. We need to get over to Alfie's to decide what to do.'

At Alfie's house the three of them sat down to get more information. There was no TV signal and the digital radio was silent. Alfie pulled down an old radio. Medium wave mainly hissed. Some sounds could be heard on long wave but were erratic and faint. He was just putting the radio back when the lights went out.

Alfie wished he'd boiled the kettle earlier. 'I knew they wouldn't be ready.'

'Could just be a precautionary shutdown,' suggested Freddie.

'That implies they had a plan,' grumbled Roger.

'Which required them to invest time and money in prevention instead of lining the pockets of shareholders. Fat chance.' Alfie humphed off to find wood for the stove.

Freddie was still struggling with the events, 'I thought they had warning systems in place.'

'Most solar storms take days to reach us. But some get here in hours,' answered Roger. 'I suspect they didn't have too much warning. They're going to need us.'

Alfie put logs onto the previous night's embers. 'Assuming they realise they need us.'

Alfie was not a pessimist but a realist, a pragmatic approach to life that he had honed to perfection since his wife had died of dementia several years earlier. The loss had not made him bitter, just wisely grumpy. 'They probably won't even know that Morse Code is still used,' continued Alfie, warming to his apocalyptic role, 'let alone know we exist.'

Roger and Freddie were quiet, partly because Alfie needed this outlet, but also because his grumpy realism often came true, even if he had been wrong about the nuclear winter.

The kettle took an age to boil on the stove but eventually they were warmed by some strong tea. Alfie stopped mid-sip.

'Lads, can you wait a while? I need to pop round to my daughter Chloe down the road. She'll be wondering what's happened. She's on her own with 3-year-old Ellie and her heating will have gone off.'

Alfie walked as fast as his bunions would allow. He knocked at Chloe's front door.

'Dad! Glad you're here. The electric's gone off so we've no heating. Can you help? I was going to go to playgroup with Ella.' Chloe pointed to the sky, 'And what's going on up there?'

Others were in the street asking if their power had gone too and staring at the strange colours, now mixing with the early sunrise. Alfie went inside and sat Chloe down to explain what was happening.

Ella was playing with a large-piece puzzle, sometimes hammering the pieces together with her fist. Alfie envied Ella's belief that all problems could be solved with a thump here and a bang there.

Chloe was looking nervous. 'I thought you were making up those solar flame things to scare the visitors.'

'Solar flares,' corrected Alfie. 'They're fairly common and usually mild.'

'Well, whatever, it looks like you were right. When will the power come back on?'

Alfie took a deep breath. 'It depends on how bad it is and how prepared they were. The real problem is when the sun throws out a huge amount of magnetised plasma – a coronal mass ejection – CME for short. That's a solar storm.'

Chloe's eyes widened, 'A storm! That sounds much worse.'

'It might last days and then they can get the power back on, but if lots of their transformers were fried it could take much longer.'

'How much longer?' asked Chloe.

'Let's not guess; just assume it'll be a few days at worst. Look, bring Ella and your things round to mine. You can sleep in the spare room. I've food put away and the stove will keep you warm. I'll put the fire guard around for Ella and I've plenty of wood in the yard.'

Chloe's fear softened to a twinkle in her eye, 'You've been preparing for this, haven't you? It's not just kitchen foil you've been hoarding, eh?'

'Well you know I like to be prepared,' admitted Alfie. 'Like the scouts and guides, only without the toggles and badges. Although if they made an "Apocalypse Preparedness" badge, I'd have several by now.' They both laughed.

He went back to get his motorbike; it could do with a good run. He filled the side car with their belongings while Chloe carried Ella and walked the short distance to his house. Ella finished hammering together another puzzle while he put up the fireguard and helped Chloe settle. The men got into Roger's car and Chloe and Ella waved them off to drive the short distance to RAF Elvington.

It was still early so traffic was not too bad, despite the failed traffic lights, and they soon reached the country roads. They were the first to arrive and unlock the main gate. The radio room was a modest space without windows, the door being the only exit. Above the room the control tower was dark, the windows reflecting the coloured sky. Lighting the stove in the radio room was the first priority, followed by checking the generator next door. They made sure all the equipment was secure in the metal cabinet, each item wrapped in black bin bags for insulation. Alfie's remaining *Star Trek* foil reflected the light from the stove and in the comforting glow they sipped their hot chocolates. They were pondering their next move when there were sharp knocks on the door. Freddie opened it to a tall silhouette.

'Well done, lads. Keen to get started I see.'

'And who are you?' asked Roger.

'Apologies. Corporal Crombie, Foreman of Signals, Royal Signal Corps,' the stranger replied, accompanied by a smart salute. Alfie unwisely whistled and got an uncomfortably long parade-ground stare in return: 'We need you lads to get some messages out using Morse Code.'

'Sorry, that isn't going to happen,' stated Roger.

The Corporal scowled a look that implied 'traitor'. 'And why not?'

Alfie wondered how many more disdainful looks Crombie had. He had been impressed that anyone had remembered them, let alone knew Morse Code could be useful in a solar storm. Now he was back into grumpy parent mode. 'Because as long as this solar storm continues, there's a radio blackout.'

The Corporal turned to someone outside the door. 'I told you it was a waste of time coming here.'

Alfie shifted into annoyingly calm parent mode. 'I didn't say the blackout would continue. It may only last a few hours, and after sunset we may get some communications back. We'll need a supply of fuel for the generator. And food. And drink. And beds to sleep on. We'll dispense with the cabaret.'

The Corporal threw his head back and guffawed. 'Done!'

By lunchtime there was no sign of the transmissions improving.

Crombie popped his head in. 'Any luck?'

Freddie shook his head, 'Nothing. This is not looking good.'

'Why not?'

'Most blackouts last a few hours at most. This has been going for almost five hours, with no sign of any let up. This could be a bad one.'

By teatime, the interference was still a problem and it continued past sunset. All Crombie could hear on the speakers was static, 'I thought it would all settle when the sun went down.'

Roger scratched his chin, 'Well, it should have if it was just a solar flare. But it seems that the solar wind is being very active and pushing charged particles past the earth. That affects the night side as well. Hopefully it will settle later.'

By late evening a few snippets of transmissions were getting through but not enough to make sense. It was past midnight before they got a brief news report from western Russia which they could not understand but recorded anyway. Crombie was intrigued and went to find someone who could understand Russian. Alexi had lived all his life in England but his Russian mother had made sure he spoke, read and wrote Russian. It had seemed second nature at first, but at school it became an embarrassment, being given the nickname 'Ruski Alexi'. When he joined the Signal Corps it became an advantage and he spent time in Germany listening in on Russian transmissions. Alexi explained that the short report had spoken of power cuts and rationing but little else.

Corporal Crombie was still looking puzzled. This was not his usual state of affairs, since army routine and discipline were his foundations, providing a high level of predictability. Field exercises brought some randomness, but essentially these were games in which routine and discipline were stalwart fellows. His wife, children and dog came next, but not always in that order.

Roger recognised that admitting ignorance was not one of Crombie's natural traits. 'You have a question, Corporal Crombie?'

'Yes. If radio transmissions are so screwed up, how come you think Morse Code will work?'

'Good question, sir.' Crombie beamed at the compliment. 'There are five levels of radio blackout, R1 to 5. Levels R4 and 5 will disrupt all signals. We didn't receive any understandable signals during the day so this must be at least an R4. As it becomes night, we face away from the sun and we're out of reach of any flares, but we're still getting interference from the solar wind. However, Morse Code is less susceptible to static than voice and we're searching the amateur radio wavelengths where Morse Code is commonly used.'

As if on cue, the speaker chattered into life with Morse Code. Freddie grabbed a pencil and started jotting down the letters. 'They don't make sense.' He showed the paper to Roger and Alfie.

Roger had a hunch. 'Corporal Crombie, could you get your Russian speaker back in here?'

Alexi looked at the letters and realised they were the Latin alphabet equivalents of Russian Cyrillic letters. 'Russian radio hams convert their alphabet into the equivalent Latin script letters and that's what they transmit. Chinese is much more challenging – they have to use a codebook where their thousands of characters are converted into a number code corresponding to its position in the codebook, and that four-digit number is what is transmitted.'

'We'll stick to easier stuff for now, shall we? What does the Russian say?' asked Crombie.

Alexi looked at the two sentences. 'He's asking if anyone knows what's happening. And he's asking if there's a war.'

Alfie leaned back in his chair. 'Perhaps he's an amateur radio ham who's getting nothing from local authorities and fears the worst. Like us, he probably went through the anxiety of nuclear war. I suspect he'd be pleased to get a reply explaining the situation. Can we send one?'

Alexi looked at Crombie who nodded permission. Freddie sent off the message and quickly got a reply which said 'Thank you.'

'I suspect he's very relieved,' remarked Alfie.

Now Europe was fully on the night side they started to get some responses in Morse Code, but the news was not good. As Alfie had suspected, not all power grids had been switched off or protected and many transformers had effectively fried. Communication satellites had been badly hit. Undersea and buried cables had been protected and fibre-optic cables were not affected, but any exposed cables and power lines on electricity pylons had received enough energy to damage unprotected transformers and equipment. The UK mobile phone system was not dependent on satellite global positioning so was unaffected by satellite damage, but even without power cuts putting equipment offline, the background noise was making mobiles unusable. Power cuts made the internet largely a dead net. With the lack of information, people were frightened, and with fear came trouble.

Much to their surprise the telephone rang.

As he was going out of the door Corporal Crombie explained over his shoulder, 'Forgot to mention. We've got the local exchange working on a generator. That'll allow local landlines to function.'

Freddie picked up the phone and turned to Alfie. 'It's Chloe. She sounds worried.'

'Dad! There are men in the street breaking down the doors of any house without a light. They're stealing anything they can get their hands on. I've put a candle in the window and I think we're safe for now, but I don't know for how long.'

Alfie started to stand up, 'OK. Stay where you are. I'll come and get you. Pack what you have and be ready.'

Outside, Alfie explained the situation to Corporal Crombie.

'No, we are not a refugee camp.'

'But it's just one person. Well, one and a bit if you count her daughter Ella,' pleaded Alfie.

'Listen,' explained Crombie. 'I'm sorry. I have family too. But I can't make the airfield a depository for displaced civilians. My section is only 12 men and we don't have the tents or equipment.' He did not tell Alfie the reality that his primary role was to protect communications, not people.

Alfie went back to the radio room to explain the impasse. Roger and Freddie returned with Alfie, each dressed in coats and gloves with umbrellas in tow.

As they walked towards Crombie, Roger casually mentioned, 'We'll be going then. Everything's switched on, just tap away and chat to whoever you want.'

'What?' shouted Crombie. 'What's the meaning of this?'

Freddie explained: 'As you can't help Alfie's daughter, we'll have to do it. Have fun. Remember to switch everything off before sunrise and put the equipment back in the cabinet, assuming you don't want fried electronics for breakfast.' They started to walk towards Roger's car.

'Wait!' said Crombie. Arrogance was a characteristic Crombie had tried to foster but he did not have the cold indifference that marked out true arrogance. He understood compromise. 'I can only spare one man and one Land Rover.'

Alexi stepped forward. 'Happy to volunteer, sir.'

'Right, Alfie you go with the Lance Corporal, on condition that the other two stay here. Agreed?'

They all nodded.

As they approached Alfie's street of terraced houses, noisy shapes ran into silent shadows, but by the time the Land Rover stopped it was eerily quiet. Alexi and Alfie jumped out as Chloe opened the door, Ella in her arms. They bundled the two in the back along with their belongings.

Alfie turned to Alexi. 'I need to get a case and something else. Drive round to the back alley. I'll meet you all there.'

Alfie went into the house, locking and bolting the front door behind him, wedging an old chair under the door handle for extra security. He damped down the stove and put a fresh candle in the window firmly anchored to a dinner plate. Hopefully the light and secure doors would discourage the moving shadows. From the cupboard under the stairs he pulled out an old trunk and dragged it through the kitchen into the back yard. He drew a grill across the back door and padlocked it, then closed and locked the door. In the shed was his trusty BSA motorcycle and sidecar which he rolled out next to the trunk. As an afterthought he went back into the shed and came out with an oil-covered cloth which he put into his coat. He opened the back gate and waited.

There were noises in a garden several doors down which he hoped was a cat. Silence returned as Alexi's headlights swung into the alley and stopped in front of Alfie.

'Alexi, give me a hand with these.'

Chloe and Ella moved to the front seat. The two men heaved the trunk onto the floor of the Land Rover. The motorcycle was more of a challenge. Alfie had had no time to separate the sidecar and it took long minutes to shove, push and jostle it on top of the trunk. Alfie took up a position sitting on the trunk next to his bike. As he sat looking out the back, the presumed cat leapt onto next door's wall. Glowing red in the brake lights was a scowling face and a large hand holding a baseball bat.

'Alexi! Get out of here, now!'

The Land Rover engine raced and jerked as Alexi threw it into gear. The man jumped onto the canvas roof and edged his way to the opening at the back. Alfie reached into the sidecar's tool box and pulled out a large spanner which he connected firmly with the squirming man above. A groan was followed by a thud as he fell into the alley behind them, rolling against some bins to the tune of much swearing.

Chloe screamed as Alexi shouted, 'Alfie, there's a bunch of them waiting at the end of the alley!'

'Don't stop!' shouted Alfie. He reached into his coat pocket for the oily rags and pulled out an old army-issue revolver. He stood at the back and aimed. Two shots over their heads scattered them like rats. Alfie heard another thump on the roof and shot through the canvas, relieved to find a plank of wood falling off, rather than a body. Alexi screeched into the road and in seconds they were on their way back. The return was in silence.

At the airfield Alexi gently helped Chloe down. He offered to take Ella, but she had every intention of staying firmly attached to her mother until all this noise and fear had settled.

Alexi helped Alfie move the bike and trunk into the store next to the radio room. 'What's in the trunk?'

'Provisions. I like to be prepared,' responded Alfie, hoping Alexi would not notice the old CND stickers on the trunk.

'Good to think ahead,' said Alexi, hoping the provisions were not as old as the CND stickers.

Crombie marched up. 'Welcome back. I won't ask why there's a bullet hole in the roof of my Land Rover Defender. I assume you had something to defend?'

Alexi saluted. 'If it hadn't been for Alfie I'm not sure we'd have got back.'

'Likewise with Alexi. You've a good lad there,' said Alfie.

'When the mutual appreciation society has finished its annual awards ceremony perhaps we could get on with the job at hand?' Crombie said with a surprising smile

'Yes sir,' replied Alexi and Alfie together.

Alfie helped Chloe set up her sleeping quarters in the control tower above the radio room. Ella was tired but would only sleep next to Chloe. 'Sorry about the accommodation, but you do have the best view in the house. At least you're safe.'

'Thanks Dad, so much. What you and Alexi did for us was wonderful.'

In the radio room they spent the rest of the night linking up to other Morse Code sites. Some were Army, but many were amateurs with generators who offered to act as go-betweens with local authorities and army units. By the end of the night they had nearly twenty UK sites and at least a dozen European ones. All through the night they could see the flickering lights in the sky and they were not surprised when before sunrise communications stopped. They disconnected the aerial, shut down all the equipment, wrapping it up in plastic bags, and stored everything in the metal cabinet. The valve equipment was less vulnerable, but they stored that away as a precaution, along with any spare valves.

Crombie popped his head through the door. 'Well done, lads. Sterling job. Looks like you all need some sleep. We'll keep an eye on everything.'

The sun was rising and they were ready to head to their beds when they heard a crackling in the corner of the room. The disconnected aerial was sparking and smoking, blackening Alfie's aluminium foil.

Crombie grabbed the fire extinguisher and was about to release it when the sparking stopped. 'What the hell was that? Did you lads leave something switched on?'

Roger realised immediately. 'Must be a second CME. This one's been slower, less powerful, but you can see what it does to exposed cables like the antenna. Now you can imagine what the first powerful one did to transformers and power lines. Fortunately we protected the equipment, otherwise everything could have fried.'

Alexi came in to say that some of the lads' radios had stopped working.

Crombie slapped his hand on the desk. 'I should have thought about that. Have you got room for the remaining radios in your cabinet?'

Roger nodded. 'You may want to check your vehicles. They may be OK as they're effectively in a metal cage, but worth checking. We'll need to check the aerial as well.'

Apart from some odd errors on the dashboard all the vehicles started normally. Crombie turned to the three men. 'OK. We'll check the aerial up top. You've done more than enough. Off you go for a rest. Thank you.'

The three men nodded, exhausted and went upstairs into an office where their beds had been set up. They were asleep in seconds.

The three were awoken by Ella jumping on each bed and shouting 'Wake up lazy bones!' at the top of her voice. Chloe ran in to pick her up, 'Sorry about that, gentlemen. She escaped. Food is ready in the mess outside.'

They got dressed, washed and shaved in the bowls thoughtfully provided by Alexi. In the mess they met Crombie.

'Good to see you all. I hope you had some restful sleep because tonight is going to be busy. We're making Elvington a communications hub and we want all your UK links to be on the same frequency. We're going to have to work out how they reply – we can't have dozens of replies coming in at once. We also need the addresses of all the amateur radio hams so we can get fuel for their generators until power is restored.'

'How long will that take?' asked Chloe.

'Not all the grids were shut down in time and some were unprotected.'

'Told you,' said Alfie, disappointed at being proved right.

'They may be able to repair some, but others will take months or longer to replace. Locally it's patchy. It may take a while. However, the UK power grid is organised like a lattice, which gives more scope for spreading the power around.'

Roger interrupted, 'You do realise we can't encode these messages. Anyone will be able to listen in, including our friend in Russia.'

'We've considered that,' replied Crombie, 'but the priority is getting communications up and running over the next few days to get some semblance of order established. If the Russians want to copy our plans, they're welcome.'

Alexi stroked his chin. 'Actually it will reassure them that we're all in the same boat and it's not some capitalist plot.'

During the night the luminous curtains in the sky continued, shifting in a dance of veils and changing colour like the surface of a soap bubble. Voice transmissions were patchy and distorted. Even the Morse Code messages had difficulty, but enough got through to make sense. They could send out instructions to everyone at the same time, but responses had to be organised on a 2-hourly rota. They allocated 4 minutes to each of the 20 sites for replies, using their individual call signs for identification. That left 10 minutes for outgoing messages and instructions and a further 30 minutes for messages to army and police on emergency frequencies. Alexi kept a log of the conversations, what information was required, and what needed to be transmitted. Alfie, Freddie and Roger took 1-hour shifts as key operator. In between they rested, took refreshments, filed messages or gave Alexi a break. If there was time they linked to some European sites, in a spirit of cooperation rather than necessity. By the morning they had helped allocate resources, passed on emergency messages and arranged support for the amateur radio operators. They had also begun to hear stories of looting, with the police and army taking control of some areas.

'We're losing the thin veneer of society,' commented Roger.

This prompted Alfie to restart his grumpy old man *persona*. 'If we ever had a veneer – more like thin tissue paper at best. Just losing the mobile phone network will have made some bereft. Hell, I've got so dependent on the damn thing I've even phoned Chloe to find out where she is in the supermarket, only to find she's two aisles down!'

'My 15-year-old nephew lives for his tablet. Obsessed with playing games with his friends,' observed Freddie. 'His mum had no idea what he was up to and asked me to look. I thought I was broadminded. What we didn't realise is that he was getting some bad messages from some so-called pals. Nasty stuff. I knew two of them and visited their parents, they were just as shocked. At least they can't get into trouble now.'

'They might have to bring back the small cinema,' mused Freddie, recalling sneaking into the old *Rialto* for the 'big picture'. He remembered sinking down low into seats covered in crushed velvet so worn it shone in the light of the flickering screen. Chewing a gobstopper was heaven, at least until the usherette caught him in her torchlight and woke Freddie from his reverie.

Freddie turned to Crombie, 'How bad is it?'

Crombie was unusually thoughtful. 'Some areas are in trouble, no doubt about that, but thanks to your hard work, troops and police are being mobilised. In fact we should have some reinforcements here today.'

Chloe looked alarmed. 'Why here? Are we in danger?'

Crombie smiled. 'Not at all. Just a precaution.'

A shot rang out.

Crombie turned and ran outside, shouting orders. Soldiers sprinted into positions carrying weapons and ammunition. The few vehicles they had were moved in a circle around the control tower as the men took up positions.

Freddie stared out the door. 'It's like being in an old Western.'

'But perhaps without the genocide, eh?' pointed out Chloe, holding Ella close.

Alexi came to the door. 'Lock and barricade this door. Don't open it for anyone except me or Crombie. Understood?'

They all nodded. Freddie could see several dozen men walking through the gate carrying weapons from bats to shotguns to spades and lumps of wood. The mob was starting to approach the control tower when Freddie slammed the door shut. Roger jammed a table against the door, each of them holding their breaths.

They could hear Crombie's muffled voice shouting a warning, followed by hesitation. That changed into a yells and gunfire. Bullets pinged against the brickwork outside and several hit the heavy wooden door with a thud. The windows upstairs shattered and there was more gunfire. Footsteps thumped up the stairs and shouting was followed by a thud on the floor. More footsteps wandered across the wooden floor. Perhaps they thought they could reach the radio room from upstairs, but it was only accessible from the outside.

Feet ran back down the steps, followed by banging on their door.

'Open this door!' commanded an unfamiliar voice. The door knob turned and rattled, then the door was kicked and shook against the table. After several more thuds it went quiet save for some indistinct shouting. The next thud had a sharpness to it that made the door shudder. At the third strike, the door splintered and part of an axe could be seen. It was levered, squeaking its way out of the wood, and hammered back with more force. It did not take long for the lock to fail. A large hooded man entered the room. Alfie recognised him as the one who had jumped onto the Land Rover. The recognition was mutual.

'You're the one who hit me the other night. Trying to protect your old pals and pretty bit of fluff were you?'

Alfie pushed to the front, but Roger held him back.

'Come on,' said the man in the doorway. 'Try me. I've an axe waiting for your head.'

Behind him they could see the soldiers kneeling on the ground, guns pointed at their heads. One was hauled upright and pushed onto the radio room floor. It was Crombie, bleeding from a head wound. He was still breathing. Roger went to help him.

'Leave him!' said the hooded man. 'He was prepared to shoot us. Us! The people.'

'But he didn't shoot you, did he?' pointed out Roger, angrily quiet.

'No! He knew when he was beat.' The man took a breath ready to launch into a polemic.

Chloe interrupted him. 'Why are you here?'

'Trying to distract me dear, eh? I'm happy to be distracted later when we're alone. But right now I'm here to defend the common man from all this.'

'What is it you need defending from?' asked Chloe.

'All this!' he pointed to the equipment. 'We don't need this technology. It's ruining our lives, giving our kids brain tumours. Just look at the sky! If the army are here this stuff's got to be important. We've got to stop you destroying us. Cutting off our power to suppress us into submission. We're not having it. You've done enough damage already with all these nightly light shows.'

So that was it, thought Roger. He thinks we created the aurora. 'You've misunderstood. We haven't caused this, it's a solar storm, from the sun. We're trying to put people in touch using Morse Code.'

The hooded man started to raise his axe. 'Do you think I'm a fool? Morse Code? Nobody uses that anymore. Look at this room. While you're sabotaging our lives, you're nice and safe. Not any more, you're not.'

Suddenly gunfire started by the main gate with the sound of vehicles, accompanied by shouting and the clanking of boots. The hooded man looked briefly behind him then turned back, the silver foil reflecting his raised axe, poised to strike. To the sound of a loud clicking buzz he froze then fell, the taser still sparking. Alexi switched off the taser and quickly bound the man's hands with plastic ties.

The reinforcements had arrived just in time. Their presence had made the attackers drop their guns and allowed Crombie's section to take back control. Alexi had taken a taser from a policemen and run to the radio room in time to see the hooded man raise his axe. Crombie was starting to sit up.

'Hell's teeth, I'm going to have a shiner in the morning. What's the damage, Lance Corporal?'

'Their aim was a bit off, so only some windows upstairs. One lad knocked out upstairs, he's being bandaged up, and you of course, sir,' reported Alexi.

'We were lucky,' said Roger.

'Partly,' explained Crombie. 'The timing of the reinforcements was lucky but the fact they got here at all was because you got the right messages through. No luck in that.'

Apart from the hooded man who was handed over to the police, the other attackers were released. Most had been frightened by events and followed the one person who had very different thoughts in his head.

'Any news on what's happening?' asked Roger.

Crombie explained, 'There's better news about the power. There are signs that the storm is easing, and once it settles we'll start powering up the transformers that are working. We may have enough running to cover at least half of the UK.'

'Aren't the power companies organising it all?' asked Alfie.

'All DNOs ...' Alfie looked puzzled, 'Distribution Network Operators are under our control. We're making sure they tell us what is operational and the decision to switch will be a central one.'

Alfie was delighted, 'Ha! You've nationalised them!'

'Not quite,' explained Crombie. 'They still own the networks and will continue to run them after the crisis but, for now, yes. Some areas will need generators for a long time, but it's looking positive.'

'I do hope the DNOs will be required to answer some difficult questions,' said Roger.

Alfie took Chloe's hand. 'You're welcome to stay at mine for the moment.'

Chloe knelt down next to Ella. 'Do you want to stay at Grandpa's for a little while?'

'Yes,' said Ella with a determined series of nods. 'Can Uncle Alexi come and visit?'

Chloe flushed. 'Maybe, yes maybe,' she said to a smiling Alexi.

Alfie changed the subject. 'I've checked the bike. It should have got fried but it seems to have been protected in the store room and it's fine. It'll get us around with very little fuel.'

'You're going to tell me next that you've stockpiled some fuel in your shed.' Chloe said with a smile.

'Just don't tell the neighbours,' replied Alfie.

'Alfie, any chance of a lift to see my nephew? He's not too far,' asked Freddie.

Alfie nodded and turned to Crombie. 'Any plans?'

'We've been tasked with staying here. It'll be a while before all communications get back to normal, so we could be around for some weeks or longer. I assume that meets with your approval, Lance Corporal?'

'Yes indeed, sir,' replied Alexi, ignoring the sniggers of some of the other soldiers.

Roger had been quiet. 'You do all know it's going to take a long time to get back to normal? It could be years before everything is up and running.' His despondence was tangible.

'Well, we've been through worse in the war,' replied Freddie. 'Roger, didn't you have an allotment in the past? Your pride and joy I seem to remember.'

'Well, yes....'

'Perhaps you could start an allotment here on the airfield and invite others to help. It might help focus people's minds as well as providing food.'

Roger beamed, imagining rows of carrots and pulling up large earthy potatoes. 'And if there's any trouble allocating peas or protecting my prize onions, perhaps Crombie's stalwart men could help?'

Crombie raised an eyebrow and gave a wry smile. 'Any trouble, we'll be there. On the dot.'

For further information about On the Dot see p270

BORROWED TIME

It had started about the time Bill's big end went.

His dear old Morris 1100 engine had started making some unpleasant clonking noises. Naivety and debt drove him to fix it himself in the hope it would get him to work. Rebuilding the 1100's combined engine and gearbox turned out to be more challenging and expensive than he had expected. He lost count of the times he and his wife Lizzie had squeezed multiple ball bearings into sprung holes onto a shaft to fit a cogwheel, only for them to fly out at all angles like rats escaping a flood.

But despite the odd leftover shim and ball bearing, the day arrived to start the engine. He had charged the battery, filled the engine with oil and water in the requisite holes, checked the connections and put on clean overalls. The attraction of having transport again eventually overcame the terror that a huge bang would tell him that the left-over ball bearing had been vital after all. His delight at the sound of an engine starting and running smoothly meant he missed the shimmer in the lights. Looking underneath to exclude an oil or water leak he thought he spotted bright sunshine outside but by the time he had got up it was the usual wet tarmac outside. He switched off the engine, and shut and locked the garage door with a satisfying smugness.

The next morning he was looking forward to getting to work without waiting for a cold bus and trying to peer through misted and dribbling windows. He got up early to check the engine, but opening the garage was a shock. His 1100, over which he had sweated and grunted, was gone. In its place someone had thought it a great joke to replace it with what looked like a pile of blankets. He pulled out his phone and dialled 999 but nothing happened. What did happen is that the top of the pile turned its face to show the superior look of a camel patiently chewing. In shock, he stumbled backwards through a rough curtain straight onto hot sand. As he turned, it was not the camel or the oven heat that anchored him to the spot, but a desert rolling into a burning sun.

Looking back, the camel blinked at him with long eyelashes and bored indifference. Its role was to go where it was told. It had already patiently put up with a cold night on a hard floor and was only briefly puzzled as to why this man had appeared. Now it just wanted an instruction to move, but for some reason the human had no idea what he was doing. The camel's blank stare gave Bill no clue of its thoughts, and he realised he had no idea what he was doing. He shuffled back across the sand to his garage, or what was now a mud brick stable containing the manure and urine aroma of a hot, bored camel. Since no-one was going to give it an order it decided to get up, a process that looked as if it was trying to work out how many legs it had and where they fitted. It then ambled out of the stable with disdain. Bill closed the rough curtain, trying to block out the impossible. In the shade it became suddenly cold and in place of the camel's stare was a pair of Morris 1100 headlights. The drive to work and the rest of the day were spent in distracted denial. He took the bus home so that Lizzie could use the car after her night shift, grateful that he did not have to be reminded of his car or garage.

Next morning's breakfast was eaten in silence.

'Are you listening?' said Lizzie.

'Sorry, distracted by the car.'

'Not as distracted as I was when I came off my shift and found you'd left the lights on again. The hospital porters had to give me a push start.'

'Sorry about that. You didn't notice anything strange about the car, did you?'

'Apart from the flat battery, no.'

He wanted to tell Lizzie about the garage, but the strangeness of the experience stopped him, if only because he was beginning to doubt it had ever happened. That doubt was quickly dispelled.

He told Lizzie he would go and check the car battery. He walked across to the line of garages and unlocked the door. All he could hear were drips of rain and distant thunder as he started to swing open the doors. He walked inside to see a pair of headlights, but his relief was short-lived as he entered a muddy tent containing two dirty motorcycles leaning against a tent pole. Despite the poor light Bill could see they were old, and wiping some mud off the tank revealed the maker, Triumph, on a long square petrol tank. He had seen pictures at the Imperial War Museum of one being used by dispatch riders in World War One. As if to make the point, the distant thunder became louder and was accompanied by orange flashes. Shells started exploding nearby. Bill quickly closed the tent flaps and the sounds went back to quietly dripping rain outside his garage. Lizzie expressed surprise that he was back so quickly.

'Is the battery ok?'

'Yes,' lied Bill.

The whole situation was irritating. Partly this was because Bill wondered if he was hallucinating and needed help, but mainly because he could not be sure how he would get to work each morning. On most days it was a normal garage with a normal car that took him to work without any noises, problems or camels. Bill decided that, if he was hallucinating, at least he could find out if it was predictable. So, late Saturday morning he decided to try the garage again, prepared to open the door as many times as it took to prove his sanity.

At the first attempt he found three sheep staring at him with eyes the colour of warm toast. He was in a small stone barn with a dilapidated thatched roof that allowed the fug to escape through blackened gaps. The rickety barn doors opened onto grassland leading to a meandering river. A small church sat quietly among some graves. The writing on one new gravestone was clear but made no sense apart from some Roman numerals. He took a photo of the grave with his phone, and then walked towards the wide muddy edge of a tidal river. Along the shore a vegetable garden was being tended by a robbed figure.

'Gréting,' said the monk with a quizzical smile.

'Hello,' replied Bill.

On seeing the monk's puzzlement, Bill responded in kind with a cheery 'Greeting!' The monk gave a beaming smile and beckoned Bill towards one of the buildings. They chatted as they walked, Bill nervous at the unexpected peace and the monk trying to put an obviously anxious traveller at ease. Neither could understand the other, although the monk giggled nervously when Bill pointed to himself and said his name. Bill waved his hands at the surroundings then shrugged, 'What's this place here?'

The monk replied, 'Hêr?' then mentioned a name that sounded strangely like 'your way'.

They walked into a low hall with a table laid out with plates and mugs. Food was arriving with other monks. The monk made eating movements with his hand and mouth while saying, 'Imete.' As Bill sat down all the monks put their hands together to say grace and then ate in silence. Many looked across to Bill and smiled nervously in welcome. The food was simple but filling. After the meal Bill sat on a log overlooking the river while the monks went to church. He rested in the quiet sunshine for a while before returning to the sheep. He closed the barn doors and was back in his own garage.

Back home Bill checked the numerals on the gravestone, DCCXXX. Assuming the dead person wasn't aged 730, it must have been the year of death. On the internet he looked up 'imete' and found it meant 'food to eat' in Anglo Saxon, while the monk's 'gréting' unsurprisingly meant 'greeting'. All that fitted with the date.

Researching 'your way' was more difficult. He tried different spelling combinations from 'year weigh' to 'yor wa'. Eventually he found that 'yeerweh' was the pronunciation for Gyrwe, the Old English name for Jarrow in the north-east of England. That fitted with the monastery there at that time. Another search explained why the monks seemed nervous on mentioning his name since 'bill' was the Anglo-Saxon for 'battle axe'. He was mulling over his new nickname when Lizzie asked what he wanted for lunch. He had assumed that it was now mid-afternoon and realised with a shock that his near 1300-year journey had taken no time at all.

'Sorry, love, shouldn't have taken those crisp packets with me.'

Lizzie shrugged and went off to have her lunch and coffee, leaving Bill to do some thinking.

The next morning Bill tried again. The Morris headlights were replaced by a pair of red eyes that followed him around like a painting in a horror film. The walls were rough rock and as his eyes adjusted he could make out hand-prints on them. The eyes belonged to a dog cowering at the back of a cave. Outside, a grassy plain stretched to a seashore. The sun was shining but the air was cold. In the distance two people were walking towards the cave, one dragging two poles with something stretched in between. They froze when they saw him. The dog trotted out of the cave. In the light it looked like a small tame wolf, which proceeded to lie down, resting its head on Bill's foot. This seemed to reassure the couple, who continued up to the cave.

Both were dressed in animal skins and fur boots. Both looked worried. In the bundle of furs between the two poles was a small girl, her face stained with tears. Every bump made her whimper. The man gently picked her up and Bill could see her left leg was bloodied. The woman cried as the man carried the child into the cave. He laid her down softly on furs and turned to light the fire. Whether because of his distress or the damp, the lichen refused to catch. Bill reached into his pocket, took out a lighter and bent down to light the lichen which fired up the kindling. He turned to the man but they were both flattened against the rock wall with a look of frightened wonder. He pointed to the stored wood and they nodded briefly.

As the flames took hold Bill turned his attention to the girl. Again he indicated if he could look at the girl's leg. They looked at each other and nodded more definitely this time, presumably impressed by his trick with fire. The girl's leg was covered with blood-soaked lichen. He removed the covering. The skin had a deep gash that had stopped bleeding but the calf was swollen. Any movement caused her to cry out. It was a likely fracture and she needed help. Bill stepped outside, hoping to find some way of getting help. He saw movement below him and the unmistakable shape of a woolly mammoth told him it would be another 150 centuries before he could call anyone.

Bill was unsure what to do. He could go home to ask Lizzie for advice, but there was no certainty he could return to help the girl. He would have to make do. Back in the cave he looked at the wood for the fire. One was straight and narrow. He placed it next to her leg and pointed to the parents that he needed another one the same size. They spoke to each other and ran outside. In less than 10 minutes they were back with an almost identical piece. He found a short piece of split wood to act as a support for her foot. Bill looked at the structure they had used to carry the girl. It was held together with leather thongs and fur straps. He pointed to these and in minutes they were handed to Bill. Using the fur to pad the wood, he tied the leather straps to the wood splints. The girl cried when they were tightened but when he was finished she was able to move more comfortably. A nervous smile appeared on her face, matched by beaming smiles from her parents.

The mother prepared some food while the father carried the girl outside to enjoy the early afternoon sunshine. Bill joined them and felt the father's hand on his shoulder accompanied by a grateful smile. The mother came out with meat seared on the fire. Bill had no idea what it was, especially as he could see all sorts of animals below including antelope and what looked like bison. But it tasted good, although vegetarian Lizzie wouldn't have approved. He imagined himself explaining, 'Well it was woolly mammoth or nothing.'

With the three outside, Bill returned to the cave intending to return home. That was when he realised there were no doors or curtains to close. They had always been the trigger to returning and he stood facing the entrance, wondering if he would get home. The thought of a lifetime of woolly mammoth fry ups was not appealing. The mother saw his frowning face, assuming it to be tiredness. She showed him the furs and with a grateful smile pulled some woven reed fences across the entrance to give him some peace. Immediately he was back home in time for lunch.

There was no sense to the type or order of places he visited, let alone why. It seemed random, with no connection between the sites, time or people and no way of controlling the visits. Although the haphazard choices were oddly exciting, he had noticed one characteristic. When his mind was on getting to work by car, the doors opened up to the usual Morris. But when he was trying to fix the car or he simply wanted an adventure he was more likely to open the doors to new sights and sounds. Two days later he was back early from work. He packed a rucksack with a torch, compass, water, first-aid kit and some food and trekked off to the garage.

He was back in the tent but this time it was night and any artillery was far away. In the dull light of an oil lamp there was only one motorcycle. The tent flap opposite flew open and a weary dispatch rider struggled in, pushing the missing bike, both of them glistening with sticky mud. A cut on his forehead was painting blood over the brown clay smeared over this face and trickling down one corner of his moustache.

'Useless pile of junk!' he said to Bill. 'Magneto packed in just as I was overtaking an ambulance. Skidded and came that close to going under the wheels.'

'Does that happen often?' Bill asked.

'The contraption dying or me being squashed by an ambulance and dying?'

'Well....' started Bill.

'Never knew Flanders could be so flipping wet. Magneto's always getting soaked around the high-tension lead. I'm beginning to wonder if the odds of a dispatch rider surviving are about the same as going over the top. Jonas slid under a lorry last week, broke both legs and got shipped off to Blighty. Lucky bastard.'

'Can't you seal off the lead?' asked Bill.

'What do you think the plasticine is for?' the man replied, clearly assuming Bill should know.

Bill had an idea. 'Where does it get wet?'

The dispatch rider took a rag and cleared away some mud around the high-tension lead. He handed Bill a dirty ball of plasticine.

'See what you can do. I need to get cleaned up and have some dinner. You coming?'

'I'll see if I can fix this first.'

As soon as the man was gone, Bill closed the tent flaps. In his garage he picked up absorbent paper towels and a tube of silicone sealant. Although he assumed these would travel with him he could not be sure if he would return to the same place. But on opening the garage doors he was back in the tent. He was about to start work when the dispatch rider returned looking cleaner and with his head bandaged.

'Missed you in the canteen. Good bit of steak and kidney. Managed a bit of kip. What's that?' He pointed to the silicone.

'A new sealant,' lied Bill

It did not take long to clear the mud, dry the area around the lead and apply the silicone with its distinctive vinegar smell.

'Reminds me of fish n' chips and pretty girls at New Brighton. Well, if it works it might save my life. Ta.'

'Happy to help.'

He left Bill to seal the other motorcycle.

The following weekend Lizzie went into town to meet a friend. Bill picked up his rucksack and headed to the garage. As the doors opened Bill's nostrils were welcomed by the smell of warm manure. The previous day he had driven front end first into the garage so should not have been surprised he was faced with the rear end of an ox. Whatever it looked like at the front, it was unpleasantly worse at the rear. Outside, the heat told him he was back in the desert but the empty sand was now replaced by a large temple gate under construction. Crowds of workers were carrying or hauling stones and mud bricks. They looked thin and exhausted. As they got closer Bill realised with a shock that many were children, some little more than about seven. Their sweat streaked the dust on their bodies and some were limping. A tall overseer with a whip made sure there was no slacking. One young boy was struggling with a hod full of mud bricks. He fell and scattered the contents. The overseer heard the noise and started towards the boy who got up and ran in erratic hops towards Bill.

He fell inside the stable, looking at Bill with terrified eyes. Bill closed the stable doors to keep the man out, but that triggered a return home. The boy was still with him, looking terrified at the sight of a Morris 1100 and a sudden drop in temperature. Bill's initial satisfaction of knowing the chasing man would only find a grumpy ox was tempered by the problem he faced of someone in the wrong future. The boy was thin and covered in cuts, bruises and scars. Keeping him here was impossible but perhaps he could help a little. He lifted the boy onto the back seat of the Morris and covered him with a blanket. As he shut the car door the boy cried out, terrified of being shut in. Bill opened the garage doors and got into the driver's seat to start the car, putting the heater on full. In 10 minutes the warmth stopped the boy's shivering. From his rucksack he pulled out some chocolate and biscuits and showed the boy he could eat these. They disappeared rapidly into the boy's hungry mouth. He indicated with his hand that the boy should stay put. He switched off the engine and went to the house to clear out the cupboards of biscuits, nuts, crisps, pasta and bread. He put them all into a sack and collected some juice and water in a large glass. On returning the boy was gone.

At the end of the garages Bill spotted the boy looking wide-eyed at the buildings in the distance and the cars roaring past in the road beyond. But when a plane thundered overhead on approach to the airport he must have thought he was being chased by a monster. He ran back to the warm car, huddling under the blanket. Bill enticed him out with juice and more biscuits. He dressed his cuts with antiseptic cream and plasters from his rucksack and waited. After 20 minutes the boy looked much brighter and Bill decided he could risk returning. He picked up the boy and went outside, closing the garage doors. On opening them again the familiar ox was back but it was now late at night with no-one around. Despite his working conditions the boy was pleased to be somewhere familiar with no flying monsters. He smiled, bowed on receiving the sack of food, and was gone into the night.

Bill walked slowly home from the garage, but any thoughts about what would happen to the boy were interrupted by how he was going to explain to Lizzie why all their biscuits had gone.

On his next trip Bill found himself back in Jarrow next to the abbey. It was one of those winter days when the smoke freezes in the still air and the lazy light softens every shadow. No-one was outside. In the empty refectory shapes danced on the walls from the oil lamps. At the far end he could hear singing echoing from a corridor, accompanied by coughing. A light flickered through a doorway and inside a young, attendant monk was mopping the brow of an old man lying in bed. Red-rimmed eyes opened and, on seeing Bill, he smiled and managed a weak 'Gréting, Bill.' before sinking back on the bed. Bill recognised him as the monk he had met many years earlier. The attending monk looked anxious at the mention of Bill's name but was reassured when Bill took the old man's hand. The hand was hot and moist and the laboured breathing was scattered with moist coughing. He looked like a dying man. To the young monk's surprise Bill smiled and left the room.

When Bill returned the young monk was relieved to see bottles in his hand rather than a battle axe. Bill had raided the bathroom at home, picking up paracetamol tablets and some antibiotic syrup one of the boys had never needed. In the monk's cell he found a chalk and slate and drew a rising sun, a midday sun, a setting sun and a moon with a line representing time. Below the line he drew two tablets and a spoon, repeating this three more times. He showed the young monk how to put the tablets and syrup in water and give this four times a day. Bill waited until late to watch the young monk repeat the medication which he did carefully and correctly. He suspected it would not work.

Bill had hoped to return to see if the old man had survived or a new gravestone had appeared, but the next trip made him forget about the monk. He had decided it was time to adjust the tappets on the car one evening, a job he probably did too often. He put on his overalls and picked up his rucksack just in case, but as he opened the garage doors he was surprised to find that was unnecessary. There was the Morris 1100, bonnet open, ready for work. He placed his torch next to the engine and was about to undo a bolt on the cylinder head cover when he heard boots outside. Turning around he realised it was not his garage. Two soldiers stopped in front of him. They were dressed in grey-green winter coats and fur hats and carried rifles slung over their shoulders. To his surprise they smiled.

'Guten Abend, Wilhelm. Es ist kalt!'

Clearly they expected Wilhelm to be working on his car. Perhaps the darkness prevented them recognising him, but to help his disguise he stroked his face, smearing it with some oily dirt from the engine. He smiled, returned to the engine and, remembering a little German from school, said 'Warm halten.' He hoped his entreaty to keep warm would reassure them and that any accent would be muffled by the engine compartment.

The soldiers laughed and moved on.

As their steps echoed down the road Bill looked around. A single bare bulb in the ceiling washed a little light on a plain 1964 calendar. All the months were crossed off until October, where the '3' was ringed heavily several times. At the back there was a door with a key in the lock, but little else. Bill ventured outside. To his left was a guard post and beyond that the unmistakable silhouette of the Berlin wall. The uniforms were beginning to make sense, as was the fact that the front of his Morris 1100 was similar to the front of the ubiquitous East German Trabant that was now in the garage.

At school Bill had been intrigued by stories of escapes and had been in awe of the courage of those who tried and often died trying. He was about to return to safer times when a couple approached the open garage. Just then a soldier walked out of the guard post. The couple ran into the garage to hide and stared wide-eyed at Bill, unsure if he would give them away. Bill put a finger to his mouth. He pulled out the dental mirror he used to look at hidden corners in the engine. He held it so he could see the guard post and waited until the soldier had finished his cigarette. He indicated the couple could leave. 'Danke,' said the man. The couple gently knocked on number 55 next door. Someone inside spoke to them and he heard the man reply 'Tokyo'. They disappeared inside.

One of the stories of escape Bill still remembered was Tunnel Fifty-Seven, named because 57 people made their escape through a tunnel dug right under the wall. He remembered the password they used because it seemed so out of place, Tokyo. More people arrived, repeating the password to be admitted next door. There were regular patrols, so some ran into the back of the garage hidden by the open bonnet. If the soldiers spoke, Bill would do his usual muffled reply. He had no idea how many escapees had gone through already but he counted at least 20 that evening. Later on, in a lull between patrols he heard the front door of number 55 open and a man came into the garage. He was covered in sand and mud and was holding a gun pointed at Bill.

'Passwort,' he demanded.

'Tokyo,' Bill replied.

The man relaxed and lowered the gun. 'Danke für Ihre Hilfe.' said the man.

Bill decided it was time to speak English. 'Happy to help.'

'You English spy? You must come back with us to West.'

'Thank you, but I have another way of getting home. I'll wait here and see if I can help others.'

The man laid a thankful hand on Bill's shoulder, checked if all was clear and went back next door.

Bill waited another hour and was about to return home when a group of five people approached. This time they were not quick enough and the border post spotted them. Bill told them to hide at the back of the garage while he looked with his mirror. Two plain-clothed men were marching quickly towards the garage. Shutting the garage doors would keep the group safe, but with no certainty of returning to their time. He ran to the back, unlocked the door and pushed them through. It led to a courtyard, in the middle of which was an outhouse. The man with the gun was waving at them to follow and they ran across to the tunnel shaft. Bill went to close the garage doors and was about to shut them when he heard banging and shouting next door. He grabbed a spanner, stuck his head out, saying 'Auf Wiedersehen,' and slammed the door shut. To his surprise the banging shifted to the garage doors and he was still in the East German garage. He realised a boot was blocking one door. This was followed by a pair of hands pulling the door open and the nozzle of a gun pushing through. He gave the boot a hefty kick and hammered a spanner down on the fingers holding the gun. There was a shout and the gun went off, the bullet embedding itself in the wall. But the garage door shut and he found himself back in his own garage. That evening he was grateful for a warm bath and was even happy to clean the oily ring from the bathtub.

For a few weeks Bill was reluctant to travel. Whenever he noticed strange lights, smells or sounds he rapidly shut the garage doors and only opened them again when they looked, smelled or sounded normal.

One warm summer evening Bill decided to have yet another go at the tappets. He tentatively opened the doors but all was normal and he walked up to the Morris, patting it to make sure it was not a camel, ox or old motorcycle. It was only when he realised the traffic noise had stopped that he looked around. Outside it was a muggy evening and he stepped out of an old stable into a small side street marked *Via dei Servi*. To his left was a confectionery of a building rising to a huge orange dome looking like the cathedral he had seen in pictures of Florence. In the distance some oxen trundled past, pulling carts. There were no cars, street lights or trappings of modern life. It seemed late and the street was deserted except for a young man staring at him. He was about Bill's age with a dark beard that was well trimmed but covered in coloured paint and plaster. The long sleeves and leggings all spattered with stains suggested either a lost stag night participant or a medieval painter and decorator. The man's sharp eyes were fixed on the Morris. For once, Bill wished it had been an ox, cart or donkey as they would have fitted into the surroundings. A shiny piece of metal with two bright eyes was going to attract attention.

The man was fascinated, caressing the smooth metal and glass windows with a beaming smile. He had started prodding the tyres when his smile changed to fear. Approaching the garage were two men dressed in black and carrying knives. The man moved to the back of the stable. Bill opened the driver's door to block the assailants' approach, then opened the car's back door and pointed to the man to get in. He did not hesitate. Bill slammed the door shut, jumped in the driver's seat and started the engine. The assailants stopped as the engine raced and the headlights glared. Bill accelerated out, scattering the men, and turned into the cathedral piazza. He had no time to think why his Morris 1100 had followed him or what it would look like in old Florence, but the man in the back seat did. He was beaming and shouting like an excited 10-year-old on a roller coaster. The only words Bill could make out were 'che', 'cosa' and 'come' repeated multiple times at varying volumes of excitement. All Bill could see were his headlights throwing huge shadows across the buildings like a demented *son et lumière* as they circled the cathedral. Some windows opened to match the open mouths of the few onlookers. Before long they were back at the stable and Bill screeched to a stop inside. To his surprise the assailants were heading towards them again. Bill leapt out of the car and closed the stable doors. The sudden cold told him he was back home.

From the car came a banging on the window. Bill opened the door and out came a smiling man.

'Meraviglioso, stupendo, fantastico!' he kept repeating.

Even if his words had made only partial sense, the look of wonder on his face needed no translation. His clothes and response to an old car suggested his Florence was well before modern technology. Bill was tempted to take him home to meet Lizzie and the children, but he suspected that television, radio, computers, mobile phones and microwave ovens would send him into overdrive, let alone planes flying overhead. Instead Bill pointed to himself and said 'Bill.'

The man was still talking excitedly, waving his arms around and pointing to himself. Bill thought he had caught at least the first part of his name and decided that would have to do. 'I'll call you Len.'

Len shrugged and smiled.

He needed to get Len back to his home, but the garage had other ideas.

The trip to Jarrow was pleasant since the old monk had survived and he met Bill like a long lost friend, comfortable with someone called 'battle axe'. Len was fascinated by a beautiful gospel that the old monk showed him while the monk in turn was entranced by some drawings that Len drew for him.

In Flanders the tent opened to a scene of devastation. In front was a destroyed trench against a backdrop of mud and tree stumps to the horizon. Injured and weary soldiers trudged past and haggard-looking horses limped to firmer ground. A motorcycle roared making one of the horses rear up. The dispatch rider saw Bill and went to shake his hand.

'Thanks for having a dekko at the bike. That fix was cushy! Despite the drizzle I managed to get the news of the armistice through. Can't thank you enough.' He then pointed to Len, saying, 'See you're ready for tonight's review then.' Bill knew he would be disappointed.

In the desert Len was fascinated by a camel resting on the desert sand. He walked around it, studying every detail. In return, the camel paid him no attention whatsoever. In the meantime, Bill waved to a young

man and a child who both ran across to him. The man
knelt down, resting his head on Bill's feet. Bill gently
lifted the head and realised he had been the bruised and
battered young boy he had helped. He reached into his
rucksack for food, but the young man shook his head
indicating he was full and proudly motioned to Bill that
the boy was his child. Behind him the city was deserted.
Whatever had happened he had made another life that
suited him well.

Len was intrigued by the wall paintings in the cave
which now included bison and mammoths. A young
woman limped outside carrying some food for an
elderly couple sitting in the sun. Seeing their smiles she
turned and her face beamed at seeing Bill. She hugged
him so tight he found it hard to breathe. This was the
girl he had helped and his smile was matched by that of
Len who was transfixed by a group of woolly
mammoths below.

Bill recognised Strelitzer Strasse in Berlin where
Tunnel Fifty-Seven had started. But the street was now
full of people shouting and dancing, heading for the
wall. Len slipped into the crowd and Bill followed. At
the wall they proceeded to hammer and bang at the
concrete which started to come down in sections. He
spotted Len who had picked up a hammer and was

joining in the mayhem with a huge grin. No-one found his long sleeves and leggings odd – they matched the carnival atmosphere. But they were not designed for the cold November chill, and after a while he spotted Bill, glad to be making a shivery return.

Finally, the doors opened into a warm Florentine evening. By the cathedral Bill could see a busy throng of people dressed like Len. In turn, Len checked they were alone in the street and spread out his arms to welcome the air of home. He invited Bill back to his studio nearby. It was full of drawings, paintings and, in the darkness, what looked like wooden models of birds hanging from the ceiling. On an easel was a drawing with perspective lines ready for more work. Len lit some candles, picked up a pen, dipped it into an inkwell and started drawing. With remarkable speed he created people, animals, shapes and scenes without stopping, totally absorbed. After an hour Len was still engrossed in his drawing. Bill crept out gently and went home.

Over the years Bill's garage no longer took him on travels. He changed cars and came to accept that his adventures had ended. He decided to write about his extraordinary journeys – 'For the children,' he told Lizzie. She thought they were rather far-fetched but was sure the boys would enjoy them and she sometimes read the stories to them at bedtime. For Bill the words reminded him of the people and places he had met. He was unsure why he had been given time with each of them except to share a kindness in that borrowed time. It seemed that each small act had created an impact far beyond the action itself. Help had a habit of spreading and growing, no matter how small the initial action.

After the children left home, Bill and Lizzie moved houses. During one move, Lizzie had been sorting out the attic and came across books and toys belonging to the children when they were young. She spotted Bill's stories and took them down to Bill.

'I'd forgotten about these,' she said to Bill. 'I'm going to read them again.'

She was intrigued by the story of the artist in Florence. Searching online she came across a drawing from 1481. It was in preparation for a painting that the artist never finished and was one of his strangest.

'Have you looked at this drawing by Leonardo da Vinci?' Lizzie asked Bill.

'Not really,' Bill lied.

'Well, it's got a camel in it.'

'So?' Bill replied.

'It's the only time he drew a camel. And there's a trench, walls, a camel lying down, a rearing horse and what looks like an elephant. But do you know the weirdest thing?'

Bill feigned disinterest, 'What's that?'

'Apart from the fact that it looks like they're all in a large garage, something odd has shown up in recent ultraviolet images of the drawing.'

'What?'

'Look on the right,' pointed Lizzie

Bill saw what looked like a square object with eyes.

'Looks like a tram. Leonardo was ahead of his time.'

Lizzie looked at him strangely, 'Or a Morris 1100?'

Bill smiled, 'Now that would be far-fetched'

*For additional information on Borrowed Time
see p271*

1: THE BOOK THAT SIGHED

Toby was bored with the stretching dullness that only a 15-year-old understands. He walked past the drifting greyness of the village, irritated by its self-satisfied quaintness. For some it offered calm reassurance but to Toby it was a throttled, suffocating blandness. He shuffled past the murky school that had nurtured his boredom into a blank absence of joy. He hurried past the damp play area that had offered little play, wet swings and scant shelter for furtive experiments into cigarettes and cider. He drifted on towards the railway station that had no trains, a memorial to lives that had stalled. After the war it had been converted into a library by stout and stalwart women determined to rebuild lives with knowledge, but who had failed to anticipate the deflation of village life into a rosy retreat from the city. Travellers had been replaced by maps, green painted benches by rows of shelves, and any steam now hissed through hot radiators. For once the old station waiting room door was open. Toby meandered in, partly out of bored curiosity but mainly for the warmth. Sleepers were no more on the railway line, but one was snoring quietly at her desk.

Miss Mary gently woke on hearing him come in. 'Hello,' she said softly. Toby grunted in response, partly thrown by Mary's smiling welcome but mainly so as not to give the impression that he was interested in anything at all.

'Can I help you find something?' asked Mary.

Toby decided this needed a response that was sufficiently vague as to have no answer. 'What you got?'

'Good question!' responded Mary, cutting off Toby's prepared reply to the usual demand to being told to get out. 'We've got fiction, literature, mystery, poetry, romance, sci-fi, thrillers, biographies, history, geography....'

'Nah,' interrupted Toby, realising she would have kept going indefinitely. 'Anything interesting?'

'Ah! It's interesting you want, is it?' Mary looked carefully at Toby with a quizzical look, then made her decision. 'You want Talking Books.'

'On vinyl records are they?' which was Toby's best attempt at an insult.

'No, they're just around a few corners at the back,' pointed Mary without a hint of sarcasm.

With nothing better to do Toby decided to follow her pointing finger. After five corners he was getting the feeling the librarian was fibbing or he had lost count of a few corners. He arrived in a warm crook of a room that smelt of dry dust. The books were all asleep in neat, parched, rows. The air had dried like a brittle hydrangea in a warm autumn shed. The gentle creaks of the worn wooden floor mingled with the slow echo of the wall clock. A little light crept past the heavy curtains, occasionally daring to spear through the faded air to produce scattered sharp flashes of light on the dust motes.

There was no other sound except for a quiet sigh behind him. Toby turned but saw only books on the old desk, its wood smoothed and polished by countless elbows. It was glowing from the light shuffling past the curtains. He was about to leave and be bored somewhere else when one of the books opened by itself.

If that was insufficient to disturb his boredom, what happened next grabbed his interest.

'Have not seen one for some time.'

'Who said that?'

'One did, naturally,' explained the book. 'Here on the desk.'

Essential to being a teenager is the ability to look stone-bored regardless of events unfolding. This implies a certain *sang-froid* that goes down well with fellow lads, although the girls thought it looked stupid. Toby put on his best marble face whose rigid pallor was doing a poor job of hiding his terror.

'What are you supposed to be?' Toby had thought about this reply. It had the right mixture of disdain and belligerence.

'One is a talking book. And an exceedingly good one if one is permitted to espouse. Did the *bibliothécaire* not explain?'

This was not the way it was supposed to work. Barbed questions were supposed to get simple angry responses that gave the excuse to be rude and, if necessary, run. Smart answers using strange words were not in the rule book, even if they came from a book.

'A book can't talk. You're a disguised iPhone, that's what you are,' Toby said in desperation, trying to see where the electronics were hidden.

'I can assure you, sir, that if I am anything, I am a Book,' the voice replied, making sure each 'I' was clearly enunciated.

'Alright, then what are you?'

'Sir, therein lies a tale. Could I suggest that sir sits down for a while?'

This was said in such a kindly tone that Toby felt he had no option but to obey. He sagged into a dusty wicker chair that creaked complaints as he settled into its comfort.

'No matter what is written, by whom or by what method, misprints, misspellings and mistakes occur. The authors assume these are erased before being corrected, but the reality is that they never disappear. They gather, accumulate and coalesce like star dust draws itself together to form celestial bodies.'

Toby felt a stirring of curiosity. 'So where do they go?'

'Why here, of course,' said the book, flicking a page to clear some errant dust off a page corner.

'But you'd end up with a jumble of wrong words. They'd make no sense.'

'Ah, but time is on their side, you see. Words from the same author tend to find each other and some order returns.'

'So who wrote you?'

'That sir is a good question... with an embarrassing answer.'

Toby wondered if the sun was setting or had the book's pages reddened slightly?

'You may remember that the words are not quite right. The words may collect around the right authors but are a little diverted from their original meanings. For example, I was written by a Charles Dickens who was writing *Oliver Twist*. Unfortunately, he had terrible handwriting so I have become... and I must offer sir my profuse apologies... *A Twist of Olive* by Carl Chickens.'

Toby thought this was hilarious and the wicker chair creaked with each laugh.

The book curled its pages in disapproval. 'It was the best the words could do, considering the state of some. You may mock, sir, but we have worked hard to retain something of our proud origins.' The book managed to look so forlorn that Toby stopped laughing, but he was struggling to clear the smile on his face.

'So, there are others?'

'Certainly,' came a chorus of replies from all the shelves, accompanied by much coughing and clearing of pages.

The released dust caused the sunlight to ripple through the air and tickle the books which squirmed contentedly in the warmth. Toby thought it looked like being underwater and was surprised to find it rather beautiful. He half expected to float gently around the shelves, but his puzzlement kept him grounded.

'How can the words find each other?'

'Quantum entanglement,' sang a duet of voices from an upper shelf.

Two books peeked over the Sci-fi shelf, enthusiastically shaking their pages. Without any sign of awkwardness the books introduced themselves:

> 'Ilack Azimuth of *I Reboot*.'

> 'Luckless Atoms of *An Itch Bikers Ride to the Galaxy*.'

They each bowed towards Toby and proceeded to explain in tandem.

> 'It started with Schrödinger's cat.'

> 'Could be alive or dead at the same time.'

> 'Particles can be linked.'

> 'Entangled, even.'

> 'No matter what the distance.'

'Presumably our words too.'

'Yes, but speaking is more difficult to
explain.'

'Have to have some mysteries.'

'Or a new theory waiting to be tested.'

Toby smiled, 'You're making this up.'

'It is what authors do.'

'If you prefer that explanation.'

'But we push the boundaries.'

'Rather well.'

'We think.'

Whatever they were talking about, Toby thought they were looking a little too smug for their own good. He thought he could catch them out. 'But computers check spelling now.'

'Ha!'

'Have you ever used a spell-check program?'

'Generate more words for us than ever.'

'I suspect the excess is driving our speech.'

'Like a word safety valve?' suggested Toby.

Ilack and Luckless stared at each other, 'That's rubbish.' 'You're rubbish.'

The two books disappeared into the Sci-fi section to have a very unscientific page-turning fight accompanied by scuffles, rustles and puffs of dust.

Toby pondered, 'You're a sort of recycling centre for words.'

'That, sir, makes more sense than the nonsense I have just heard from those two.' Carl raised his eyes in exasperation at the dust clouds above.

Those two stopped arguing, looked down peevishly and started discussing the virtues of recycling versus quantum theory.

A quiet female voice gently interrupted, 'You seem somewhat overwhelmed, master Toby.'

'What do you expect? I'm having conversations with books. I'm supposed to read you, not the other way round.'

'Yes, it can be disconcerting for a young gentleman such as yourself.'

'And how come you know my name?'

'Mary the librarian mentioned you, so we knew about you before your arrival.'

Now that was disconcerting. What else did they know? Teenagers always had some awkward secrets that went with awkward legs and spots.

'Fear not, master Toby. I can assure you we know nothing more. Let me introduce myself. I'm Elaine.'

'Not sure I can place the book.'

'Elaine Frosting of *Bride Perfectionist.*'

Seeing Toby's persisting puzzlement she added, 'Jane Austin? *Pride and Prejudice*?'

'Wasn't that a TV series with some bloke getting wet in a lake?'

'I think you will find it was a book first. And Mr Darcy never did anything so vulgar in our book,' said Elaine rather primly.

'Perhaps the TV writers used some of your lost words?' suggested Toby.

'Certainly not.' If a book could give a haughty look, the straight, stiff spine had the same effect. 'Once we are written, we take no responsibility for how others choose to adulterate our prose.'

'Do TV and film writers have similar problems with their words?' wondered Toby out loud.

Ilack and Luckless peeked over the top shelf again.

'Not when they leave out half the story.'

'And change the rest.'

'So it doesn't make sense.'

'And leaves nothing to the imagination.'

The last was said in all innocence, but it meant something different to a teenager. 'What do you mean?' whispered Toby, hoping to hear a juicy secret.

'Words create sparks.'

'Sparks create light'

'That let you see a world.'

'Your world.'

'No-one else's.'

'That makes words more real than any picture.'

'I must say, I agree,' proffered a book surrounded by a soft haze. A long clay pipe was sticking out and gently wafting out a sweet cloud. The book was leaning back casually and, to complete the image, a couple of book marks slid out like a pair of comfortable wool slippers.

'I have seen the power of words build kingdoms of past and future, good and evil, more easily than my pipe smoke rises to the ceiling. A stream of words becomes a sea of invention; a lattice of sentences becomes an ocean; a matrix of tales becomes a universe....'

'And too much smoke makes us giddy,' chastened Elaine, coughing demurely by curling a page over herself.

Elaine turned to Toby. 'This is Jarr Talkin whose surname is very apt since his loquaciousness is presumably an attempt to counterbalance the title of his book, *Bored of the Things*.'

'Wait,' said Toby. 'I'm getting the hang of this. I've seen your films, *Lord of the Rings*. Hobbits, wizards and orcs.'

'I can assure you they are not *my* films. Anyway my version has Dobbits and Auks, quite different.'

'And the wizards?' asked Toby.

'Well, my wizards are the sort that do card tricks at dinner tables. Less impressive but less likely to get you killed.'

Toby didn't feel that Talkin's version would have the same impact as the original but, uncharacteristically, he decided that he looked so at peace with the world that he did not want to upset him.

Toby noticed the section marked Economics containing some shifty looking books. It was difficult to know why they looked so furtive, except they avoided Toby's gaze and twitched their spines while trying to retreat into the shadows.

'Why are they looking like that?' Toby asked Elaine.

'It's not their fault. They were meant for other sections but they were caught out by Economics. Until their words finally get together, this is where they have to stay.' She introduced each one in turn.

'Forge Allwell's *Nineteen and Fourpence* has become a dark tale of a sales strategy wherein nothing sells for more than one pound. Belfry Chancer's *Canterbury Sales* is a morality play of post-Christmas shopping and Danny L. Tofu's *Robins on Cruises* compares travel costs. It could take a while before they get closer to their originals.'

Each book briefly bent a spine and looked at Toby, before disappearing as furtively as they had arrived.

Toby was puzzled. 'Elaine, how come you're looking at me with your pages open and those books were looking at me despite being closed.'

Elaine smiled coyly, 'We have several faces that are read; our spines, our covers and our pages. You could say we have very expressive faces.'

Toby thought about this. 'So when you tell children you have eyes at the back of your heads, you really mean it.'

'Yes, there's no going behind our backs.'

Toby sank down into the wicker chair which crackled contentedly. Much to Toby's surprise he had enjoyed this trip into literature's recycling centre, but it was getting late and there was only so much a teenage brain can take in at one time. He rose to leave, muttered goodbye and turned away. As he rounded the first corner the books sighed. It was always like this. The few that came, looked, decided it was all an illusion and never came back. Toby stopped and returned to the warm corner. All the books turned their pages towards him, surprised at his return.

Toby looked at the books and surprised himself by saying, 'Can I come back?'

'You would be more than welcome, but may I presume to ask why?' asked Elaine.

'Your words are more interesting than most I've read.'

'Thank you, sir.'

As Toby left, the sigh that followed him was one of contentment.

For additional information on The Book That Sighed see p273

2: THE BOOK THAT DIED

It was not a pretty sight. The book was lying face down on the floor, a pen sticking out of its spine. Dark ink crept from under the pages and oozed across the floor to join pages ripped out and tightly crumpled.

Toby had been looking forward to meeting the books again. He admired their mixture of pride and eccentricity, making the best of leftover words and misspellings. But it was different this time in a way the approaching winter outside could not explain. The library air was still warm but it felt heavy and burdened. He was met by Mary, the ever-present librarian whose smile of welcome failed to hide her red eyes and wet cheeks. She could only manage a whisper and point.

'Please help.'

The welcome tidiness of the library had been replaced by a harsh mess. Books were scattered across the shelves and desk in a disorder that would have horrified even the most languid librarian. The hissing from the radiators was competing with multiple whispers but, as Toby entered, this hushed to an occasional sob. He saw a book on the floor with a pen sticking through its spine.

'What happened here?' asked a shocked Toby.

'She wasn't in the right category,' said one voice.

'She didn't deserve this,' said another.

Toby was no wiser. A book peeped past a bookend.

Tabitha came forward. 'I may be able to help. A book has been taken from us.'

'You mean someone's borrowed it?'

'Not unless it's a very long-term loan.' Tabitha pointed to the floor. 'She's dead. And very murdered.'

'She?'

'Yes. And why not? You are not an "it" are you?' retorted Tabitha indignantly.

Toby was unsure if that mattered. 'Which book was it, I mean she?'

'She was *Murdered in the Orientated Press*.'

'More like she was murdered in the library with a dagger. Colonel Mustard was it?' Toby's grimace was met with a stony silence. Perhaps they never played board games.

'I think we need to talk,' Tabitha said coldly and pointed with a page to the wicker chair. As Toby sat down the chair expressed its displeasure at Toby's attempt at humour by refusing to make any noise at all. He found the chair's refusal to creak more unsettling than the silence staring at him from all the shelves.

'I'm Crispy.'

'I suppose it's the heat?' suggested Toby, once again failing miserably to lighten the mood.

'No,' she replied calmly, 'I'm Tabitha Crispy. My author, Agatha Christie, wrote the original for the book you can see prostate on the floor.'

'What? *Murder on the Orient Express?* Saw the film. Good it was. They all did it. But, if she's dead down there, which book are you?'

'My author did write other books. I'm *Death on the Pile.*'

'Seen that film too. Bloke with a moustache solves it. Didn't think it was on a carpet though.'

'Well, that's the misspellings and misprints for you. It gives the librarian headaches trying to classify us.

That's why the murdered book was in Current Affairs. She should have been in Crime Fiction with me, but the title put her in News.'

'I think you'll find a pen sticking out of her back put her in the news,' joked Toby in one last, desperate attempt to lighten the mood.

'Not funny,' retorted Tabitha, putting an end to Toby's attempts.

Toby tried to regain some composure 'How can you murder a book?'

'We didn't think you could. We've had occasional accidents over the years. A child wandered in, took Leo Tolstoy's *War and Peace* and threw it on the fire. Took ages to burn. But it came back, albeit as Theo Toaster's *Bore and Grease*.'

'Zdravstvuy!' exclaimed a weighty tome hiding on the bottom shelf of the Engineering section. 'At least I am safe here from pyromaniacs,' a booming voice grumbled. He immediately went back to work on a broken book end. Theo liked to keep busy by fixing things in dark, safe corners.

'You need a sleuth, a detective,' suggested Toby.

Tabitha tried to sound modest. 'I have been known to solve a few crimes myself. But I have some help.'

'Sir Parfour Donald Coil at your service, sir, madam.' announced a book earnestly. It was already flicking through its pages, sifting the facts and giving the impression of a substantial moustache on a portly frame. 'My author's Mr Holmes would have solved this in a trice, but my place in the Travel section as *Gairloch Homes* means you must make do with my services.'

Tabitha looked respectfully at Sir Donald, 'I'm sure your expertise will be invaluable.'

Two polite voices from the Travel section joined the discussion. 'We would find it most advantageous to provide you with assistance, if that is acceptable and does not incommode you in any way.'

'Thank you both.' Tabitha turned to Toby and explained 'These are the Bronty sisters.'

'Merrily Bronty of *Withering Sights*,' said one.

'Sharlot Bronty of *Plane Air*,' piped the other.

'Delighted to make your acquaintance,' said Merrily.

'Likewise, I am sure,' said Sharlot.

Each held out a soft page edged in white lace. Toby gently touched the outstretched pages.

Tabitha smiled. 'Don't be fooled by their politeness, Toby. These girls are sharp, tough and resilient. They will make excellent allies in our hunt for the truth.'

The Bronty sisters smiled demurely, but closed their covers with a snap loud enough to make it clear that no-one messes with the sisters.

Toby looked around, 'Is there anyone else who wants to help?' The only reply was an awkward shuffling of pages.

Tabitha explained, 'They're frightened. Nothing like this has happened before. Some like Theo are hiding; others have found other ways to forget.'

A slurred voice drifted up from a lower shelf. 'Rrubbisshh. Not forrget nuffink.'

Tabitha leaned towards Toby and whispered, 'That's Alex Hummus,' as a dishevelled *The Three Dusky Beers* fell off the shelf onto the floor and started snoring with occasional hiccups as an accompaniment.

Tabitha, Toby, Sir Donald, Merrily and Sharlot. It was their shared strangeness that bound them.

Toby looked at the gathered company of sleuths. 'Looks like it's just the five of us then. Where do we start?'

'Could I suggest with the facts?' remarked Sir Donald. 'We have a death. But we do not know why.'

'Being stabbed in the back may have had something to do with it,' suggested Toby.

Sir Donald ignored him. 'We share a loss. We need to expunge the grief. But we can only start to do so once we understand the events from the beginning. What do we know about our victim?'

Tabitha explained, 'For obvious reasons I knew Agnetha well.'

Toby couldn't help himself, 'Agnetha?'

'When the same author has several books we use variations of the name. I think hers came from a Swedish pop group. She liked listening to music on the radio; she said it gave the words colour.'

'How did Agnetha seem in the days before she died?' asked Sir Donald.

'Sadness seemed to follow her in the last few months, but she never said why.'

'Then that is where we should start,' suggested Sir Donald. 'Merrily and Sharlot, could I ask that you speak to your friends in the Travel section? Tabitha, could you speak to your associates and colleagues in Fiction? I would like to examine the body and then I may have a chat with Theo in Engineering.'

Toby felt an urge to put up his hand, 'What can I do?'

'Could you speak to Mary the librarian? She may often seem asleep, but I have never known her miss anything and she knows the library well. Perhaps there was something unusual in the comings and goings, sparse as they are. Can we all meet here for tea?'

Like meerkats scattering at an alarm call the group disappeared into the various corners and shelves, leaving wisps of dust hanging like funeral drapes over the grisly scene. From under the desk Sir Donald observed every detail. The lingering smell of perfume. The small broken clock stuck at quarter past seven. The pages torn from the book, crumpled tightly and discarded. The intricately carved inkstand in the corner, lying on its side, next to the upturned inkpot which slowly continued to empty its dark contents under the body. Agnetha lay facing the floor, pages outstretched as if she was flying. Only the stillness of the pages showed that life had left its words. The pen was deeply embedded and had entered with enough force to break her spine. Gently, he lifted up some pages to see how far the pen had penetrated. His 'Ahh!' of surprise was less at the fact the pen had gone right through her body, but more at the way the leather was curled around the handle and the state of the nib. He stood back, looking at Agnetha's fallen form, when he noticed the front cover and was surprised for a second time. He made a note of each detail and went to look for Theo.

Toby spoke to a still-trembling Mary, the cup and saucer tinkling in her hand. She was sure that, apart from Toby, no-one had entered or left that day.

'I was relieved to see you, Toby. Early this morning I thought I heard a shout followed by a thump, then nothing, but otherwise it's been too quiet. I have also spoken to the library and it is sure that nothing unusual had happened.'

'Why would you phone the Central library? Have they got cameras in here or something?'

'This Library is self-aware,' stated Mary as a self-evident fact. 'It is difficult to know which came first, the words or the Library, but they work together. Ask the Library a question.'

Toby wasn't sure why this seemed stranger than everything else here, but he looked around and asked, 'What did I have for breakfast?'

Near the ceiling corner a shadow broadened into a scowl and a Shakespearean voice echoed around the walls.

'*The mundanity of your question does not deserve a response.*'

'What's the matter, too snooty to speak to a real person?' said Toby, warming to the argument.

'*A real person would show respect for his superior.*'

'A real library would know that silence is the rule,' retorted Toby.

'*Touché. You had toast with marmalade.*'

'Smartarse,' The scowl in the corner became a grin. Toby was surprised that he was relaxed about speaking to a ceiling. But on reflection if you could have talking books, why not a talking library?

Mary interrupted the conversation. 'Do you think we will ever find out what happened?'

'I hope so, you have good people working on it. Maybe smartarse here can help?'

'*Perhaps.*'

Agnetha had been kind to Tabitha when she arrived. She had helped Tabitha adjust as her pages filled and helped her to make the most of the mistakes and errors. Like Tabitha, Agnetha was proud of her origins, but the spent words could change lives. Books had limited control over their words. They could nudge some into place, but however hard they tried, their version would always differ from the original. Few thought they had improved on the original, although Zenith Mayhem of *Wine in the Pillows* was sure his version was much more fun. Some, like Tabitha, remained close to the original with only modest changes. Others adapted to their new roles.

Merrily and Sharlot were delighted with their reassigned status in the Travel section, having always wanted to learn more of the world. A few, however, found their words converging into a mockery of the original. Agnetha had struggled with her version, especially when she was reclassified to Current Affairs and felt that she was being exiled into the fluff of sensationalism.

Merrily and Sharlot had started interviewing their neighbours in the Travel section, but apart from picking up tips on visiting libraries in Europe, they had learnt very little. The books had heard a noise, but that was all. They decided to travel up the shelves. Again there was little to learn. Some thought they had seen a shape fall past them, but little else. It was very different in the Current Affairs section on the top shelf. Here the books were frightened, cowed into corners. Merrily and Sharlot split up and started interviewing the inhabitants. They met at the front edge of the shelf. Directly below them was Agnetha's body.

Merrily leant over the edge. 'It seems likely that she fell from here, but they all deny seeing anything. Are they all lying?'

'Only one needs to be lying. But I heard odd rumours.' replied Sharlot.

'So did I. Someone was stealing their words.'

On cue, they all met around the librarian's desk. Mary had prepared tea and some small cakes with icing that spelt 'Eat me'. A Mr Louis Carole regularly baked them for Mary which they thought was very amusing, although she recognised that his belief that they would make him smaller (or at least thinner) was a delusion. In the corner of the ceiling the Library was keeping an eye on the gathering. Toby thought it was a little distracting to have a single eye looking at you, especially as it really did follow you around the room. Sir Donald and Tabitha stood together, Sir Donald flicking through his notes and Tabitha curling her pages in thought.

Sir Donald began, 'This terrible event has all the indications of a callous and vicious murder.'

'Except for the facts,' interrupted Tabitha.

'Indeed the facts,' continued Sir Donald. 'She was not murdered on the shelf.'

'Nor on the floor,' added Tabitha.

Toby was puzzled. 'Where then?'

'It only seems puzzling until you see the evidence,' explained Sir Donald. 'The pen was the first clue. Toby, here is a pen. Could I prevail upon you to pretend that you are going to stab me?'

Toby picked up the pen, gripped the handle and lifted it in the air, ready to strike, with the shrill of the film *Psycho* echoing in his mind.

'There! He is about to stab me and the nib is aimed at my title page.'

Toby waved the pen about. 'What's wrong with that?'

'Two facts. Firstly, the nib in Agnetha is damaged and covered in ink but without any paper fragments, so the nib cannot have penetrated through her spine. Secondly, the leather over her spine is bent outwards showing the pen went in handle first, from the front.'

Tabitha looked at the others. 'That requires considerable force, much more that even you could provide Toby. I suspect there is more to this story.'

'Indeed there is. Merrily and I spoke to many of Agnetha's neighbours and uncovered an unpalatable truth.'

Sharlot explained: 'Someone had started to steal words from the other books in Current Affairs. We suspect it was Agnetha. The words only went missing after she had visited individuals. Sometimes there were gaps in their text and on one occasion part of a page had been cut out. Then there was her title.'

'Indeed,' said Sir Donald. 'The title was the second clue. It had changed to *Murder in the Orientated*

Express. The last word was not what she was given when she arrived. I must confess to having failed to recognise its importance until the Bronty sisters put it into context. My thanks, ladies.'

The sisters fanned their pages with pride and a little embarrassment.

Toby tilted his head towards Tabitha, 'How do you steal a word?'

'Our books have long been known to exchange words if that helped both parties, but we have never known words to be taken without permission.'

Sir Donald continued, 'And then there was the perfume. Was she meeting someone?'

The deep silence was interrupted by an equally deep voice from a book on the top shelf where it had been listening to the conversations.

'Yes, me.' For such a hefty volume Theo was surprisingly agile. He jumped down onto the desk with a menacing thud.

'Forgive me,' said Sir Donald, 'but I invited Theo. I felt he would be able to make sense of our quest for the truth. Please tell everyone here what you told me.'

After his dramatic entrance Theo sank down onto the desk with a deflated sigh. He looked at each of them

'I can see you believe me to be the murderer, but I loved Agnetha and would never have harmed her. I knew she was sad about her words, but I saw a beautiful and brave soul trying to make the best of her life. We wondered if we could write some replacement words so I carved her an inkstand. Mary kindly let me have a pen and ink.'

He looked at Mary whose smile was joined by a tear.

'Agnetha would visit me in the Engineering section below and we would toil together. At first it seemed to work, but over time many of the transferred words faded and disappeared. Agnetha became increasingly despondent.'

Tabitha laid a page on Theo's spine. 'What happened?'

'The night before, an angry Agnetha had pushed out the inkstand onto the floor, saying she had had enough of new words. I had hoped she meant she had come to accept her situation but in the morning I could hear sobbing from above. I ran up to the top shelf to find Agnetha tearing out her pages and throwing them on the floor. I shouted to her, but she smiled, opened her pages like wings and gently floated over the edge. There was a dreadful thud and as I looked over I could see she had fallen onto the upright pen. I should have stopped her, seen her desolation.'

Tabitha comforted Theo who had sunk into a quietly sobbing heap. 'We all failed to realise how desperate she was.'

Sir Donald explained, 'So Agnetha was not murdered, but perhaps, like her book, we each bear some of the burden.'

'What will happen to her now?' asked Toby.

Mary looked up. 'I will look after her. It is my job after all. Who knows, perhaps new words will come and bring life to her again. In the meantime she will be safe with me.'

Mary rose to fetch Agnetha, then hesitated and turned towards her friends.

'Her tragedy is shared between us, and while it is sad she was never able to share our happiness, the real tragedy is that she was never able to share her sadness. We must not let that happen again.'

3: THE BOOK THAT LIED

It was hard enough going through life as you, without pretending to be someone else.

Toby had decided to visit the Library on the way home from school. Mary was doing her usual impression of being fast asleep. Her glasses had slipped studiously onto the tip of her nose and her lips wobbled as she exhaled a dainty snore. A slight wetness at the corner of her mouth knew better than to extend into an impolite dribble. A slender hand supported her librarian bun. Her little finger twitched slightly as she dreamt of a hunky book lifting itself from a lake, his soaked dust cover transparent against the well tooled leather....

Mary awoke suddenly, looking a little flustered. 'Hello, young master Toby. How can we help you today?'

'I was wondering if some of the books would let me read them?'

'I doubt they would allow you. How would you like someone rummaging through your clothes?' Mary had an oddly faraway look. 'However, they are always happy to read to anyone willing to listen,' she added quickly before anyone could guess what was on her mind.

Toby trundled round the usual five or perhaps six familiar corners. He had got used to the Library's habit of changing shape and suspected it did it out of impish delight. Not surprisingly for a section on talking books, they were busy exchanging words, debating ideas, chatting about new developments and cleaning. Toby had never seen the Library so tidy. Even the dust particles were looking for a new home and, as he dropped his rucksack on the floor, not a mote was displaced.

A smiling Tabitha met him. 'Welcome again, Toby. What can we do for you today?'

'Mary said one of you might be willing to read me your stories.'

'What are you looking for?'

Toby briefly pondered games, girls, spots and food, but he suspected Tabitha was expecting something that might infuse a little improvement into his bored adolescent mind.

'Anything on self-improvement?' suggested Toby.

A book was already bouncing up and down in the Health section, sticking out a page like an eager primary schoolchild who knew the answer to 2+2.

'I think we have a volunteer,' smiled Tabitha with an eyebrow more raised than the comment deserved.

The book bounced down onto the desk.

'Excellent choice!' he said, despite the fact he had not been chosen. 'I am Hector and I would be happy to share my *oeuvre* which is entitled *Get the Power Monkeys To Scratch your Back*. My subtitle is *Mindful of Loch Ness*, although I suspect that part may have got muddled in the transfer.'

Toby had no idea what any of the titles meant. 'What book are you from?'

'It seems that misprints and misspellings from self-improvement books are rather numerous and I seem to have collated many such books, but there is only one of me in this library.' Toby was beginning to suspect one was going to be enough.

With more amusement than seem warranted, Tabitha said, 'Have fun.'

Toby was unsure how much fun this was going to be, but Hector was undeterred.

'With my help you will throw off the shackles of modern life, live at peace with yourself and see the world with different eyes.'

Toby thought sunglasses and some cider could do all that. But perhaps a little less stress would be good. Just getting up was stressful. He never understood why people liked the sunrise when waiting for winter brought it to you at a sensible time. It also annoyed him that those arriving early were praised for their enthusiasm, but no-one ever noticed when he stayed late. 'OK, what do I have to do?'

Hector was looking a little too enthusiastic for Toby's liking. 'First we will look at fighting stress.'

While the concept of relieving stress made as much sense to Toby as trying to make politics kinder by hugging a politician, Toby wasn't sure that fighting was going to make him feel less stressed.

But Hector was in full flow:

'We start by breathing.' His pages arched around his sides. 'In, one two three. Out, one two three. Continue. In through the nose, out through the mouth. Purifying air in, toxic stress out,' Hector intoned in a voice that was meant to be relaxing but sounded soporific.

After a dozen excursions of breath, Toby was looking pale. 'I'm starting to feel dizzy.'

'Perhaps a little too much out,' suggested Hector. 'We will try a little relaxation. Sit in the chair.'

While Toby was settling in amongst the wicker chair's customary groans and creaks, Hector went over to the Natural History section. He came back with *Glue Gannet Goo* which was still largely about the natural world and written by a famous TV naturalist but one who practised ventriloquism as a hobby. Hector whispered 'Oceans' and the book opened up to a two-page view of the Pacific, accompanied by the sounds of soft waves and distant whales.

'Just relax and let each part of your body feel heavy.'

He started by instructing the toes to relax and worked his way up. By the time he got to Toby's neck, the repetitive, monotone voice had convinced Toby that Hector had a depressive illness serious enough to require immediate admission and treatment.

'Are you feeling ok?'

'A little tired. Perhaps we could continue tomorrow,' admitted Hector.

Toby left Hector listening to waves and whales. Passing the librarian, Mary commented, 'Did that help?'

'Not yet,' said Toby, 'not yet.' Mary smiled.

The next free weekend Toby got up early enough to surprise his parents and his brother in their dressing gowns. They had always believed a good breakfast to be essential to life, but Toby turned down the offer of a full English which only seemed to promise a full coffin. His mother's alternative of muesli and nuts always gave Toby the sensation of having eaten half a pound of lead. She had suggested some superfoods, but chips, cakes, chocolate and biscuits were all super as far as Toby was concerned. Toby escaped with coffee and a croissant, mainly because they seemed mysteriously continental.

Hector was waiting when Toby arrived. 'I have made a list of strategies for you. A Toby Try-out Tour, if you like.'

Toby suspected he wouldn't like. 'What do you have?'

Hector went through his list.

Running was good for you, Hector maintained, but Toby had seen too many runners looking as if they were about to have a massive heart attack. It did not look like a fun way to die.

Hector suggested getting a cat would ease stress. Toby's Aunt Eddie had a cat that purred all day on the sofa demanding only food, milk, warmth, shelter and the right to drop small animals on the carpet, some still alive. There seemed nothing relaxing about Aunt Eddie's cat.

Hector tried to explain mindfulness, but this made no sense to Toby who felt his mind was already too full and he could see no reason to cram more in.

Looking at Hector's pictures of yoga, Toby thought it seemed suitable only for super supple people with nothing better to do than make their limbs into strange pasta shapes. Toby already knew that eating pasta was much more comforting, even if it reduced his suppleness in places.

'You're not really finding this helpful, are you?' suggested Hector.

'I'm just finding it difficult to find something that makes sense to me.' explained Toby. 'What did you find most helpful?'

To Toby's surprise, Hector burst into tears and shrank into a corner of the Nursing section. Toby placed a soothing hand on his sobbing spine, but this was quickly brushed aside by the starched white pages of a nursing manual whose determination to help removed any need for a blue flashing light. Toby stepped back.

'Step aside, young man!' she said unnecessarily.

As she carefully lifted Hector's page to check his pulse, Toby could read her front cover, *Votes on Nursing* by Flo Night in a Gale.

'Have you quite finished staring at my front? Get this man a hankie!'

Flustered, Toby searched his pocket and handed Flo a paper tissue, hardly used.

'If I had wanted used blotting paper, I would have asked for some.' Flo dropped the tissue as if it contained plague. From a back page she pulled out a spotless white cloth and proceeded to wipe Hector's tears. This had the desired effect and Hector's sobbing settled into an occasional hiccup accompanied by a smug smile from Flo.

Tabitha joined them, having heard the noise and Flo's commands.

'Is everyone alright?'

'Certainly not. This young man has upset dear Hector.'

Toby was clearly upset at the turn of events. 'I - I didn't mean anything. I only asked what he found most helpful to ease his stress.'

They turned towards Hector, but he had disappeared.

Long after Toby had returned home, they searched every corner of the Library. This was made more difficult because the Library had more corners than logical geometry allowed. Some corners had an annoying habit of disappearing, precisely because it had more than its fair share of corners. This surfeit never bothered or embarrassed the Library since it liked to think it had cornered the market. This gave it an air of annoying smugness. On occasions it thought it fun to see someone navigate four right-hand corners but end up in a different room, or pass three left-hand corners and one right-hand corner, only to end up where they started. Most times it was content to allow individuals like Toby to reach their destinations, but this time it was puzzled. Despite searching even the most ethereal corners, it could not find Hector.

Over dinner that evening Toby's mum asked him what sort of day he had had.

'None of your business,' said a voice from the hall behind Toby.

'What did you say?' asked Toby's dad. 'Don't speak to your mother like that!'

'I didn't...,' started Toby but stopped when he recognised the voice. 'Sorry mum. It was interesting.'

His parents assumed this meant school had been productive, but Toby was not about to tell them the truth. 'Please may I leave the table?'

Impressed by this sudden flowering of good manners, they agreed. Toby ran out, picked up the rucksack and disappeared up to his room. He opened the bag and stared in. Hector stared back.

'What are you doing in there?'

'I needed somewhere to think. Your bag was nearest.'

Toby sat on his bed. 'I'm sorry I upset you.'

'Not your fault, it's me, but I don't really want to talk about it.'

Toby changed tack. 'I didn't know the books could leave the Library.'

'Neither did I.'

'I thought you'd burst into flames or get dragged away by demons on passing the Library threshold.' Toby imagined dark shadows reaching out to pull the errant book into the abyss like the villains in *Ghost*, not that he would ever admit to having seen such a soppy film.

'You've been watching too many films,' Hector guessed with creepy accuracy.

They settled down to watch *The Shawshank Redemption*. Hector watched Andy Dufresne escape prison through a sewer pipe and realised he had been lucky to get out of the Library in a warm, dry bag. As they turned in for the night Hector remarked, 'I'll keep an eye out for monsters.'

'You've been watching too many films,' said Toby but, in truth, he was pleased to have someone who would look out for... things.

From inside the rucksack a book smiled.

The next morning Toby got ready for school.

'If you like I could drop you off at the Library after school.'

'I'd like that, but can I make a request? Can I come back?'

'Deal' Toby gave a high five to ten raised pages.

Hector promised not to make any comments over breakfast and was content to peek out of Toby's rucksack on the way to school. He was not impressed by what looked like masses of disorientated lemmings, each scurrying towards their personal cliffs, focused only on the inches in front of their feet. He thought they had far too many Power Monkeys on their backs.

On the bus Hector kept hearing 'pops' on the rucksack as if it was raining. Peeking out through a gap he noticed some boys chewing paper into pellets and blowing them through straws at Toby's head. 'What are they doing?' whispered Hector.

'Nothing, keep quiet,' shushed Toby.

When they arrived at the school the same boys caught up with Toby in the cloakroom. Hector felt something hard hit him, followed by Toby falling to the ground. A boy with a snotty expression jumped on Toby's back and demanded he hand over his lunch money. When Toby failed to reply he launched punches at Toby's face. Hector saw his chance. Unzipping the rucksack, he reached out, pages open, and closed them with a crunch on the assailant's nose. The boy sprang back with blood starting to run down his lip. All he remembered afterwards was a wide grin disappearing back into Toby's rucksack, an image that recurred like a nightmare each time he saw Toby. He turned and ran. The others followed, impressed at how Toby could punch so accurately behind his back.

'Thank you, I don't know what you did, but thank you.'

'No problem. To be honest, I haven't had this much fun in ages.'

On the way back from school Toby and Hector visited the Library. As he passed Mary, she wondered why Toby was smiling until she spotted a wide grin from inside his rucksack. 'A warm welcome back, Hector.'

'And to you too,' said Hector with a spring in his voice that gave Mary a warm smile.

Even the Library was pleased, allowing Toby and Hector to travel past only one corner before arriving in front of a group of anxious faces.

Flo pointed angrily at Toby with a well starched page 'How dare you kidnap dear Hector!'

'Flo, dear,' interrupted Hector, 'it was my decision to get into Toby's rucksack. He knew nothing about it until he got home.'

'But why?' Flo seemed less than her usual prim self, softer perhaps.

Hector looked down at his footnotes and said, 'I have a confession to make. All these wonderful theories and treatments that came my way seemed so sensible. I told people how they worked and why they worked.'

'What's wrong with that?' asked Flo.

'I allowed everyone to think I had tried them all.'

'What... not even the yoga?'

'None of them.'

'So you...,' Flo could not bring herself to continue.

'Yes I lied.' admitted Hector.

There was a silence. Then Tabitha spoke up.

'To be honest, Hector, we all suspected. What mattered is that you believed in it.'

'Well, it mattered to me,' said Flo, looking up with a slowly spreading grin. 'I dare not say what some yoga positions did to my digestion.' Everyone smiled.

'I just wanted you to feel positive about yourself.'

Flo looked at Hector and gently rested a page on his spine, 'But being positive all the time is like expecting a battery to work without a negative end. You can't switch on a light unless you have both.'

'That makes more sense than the stuff I was peddling. I'm going to try for a re-write, perhaps with a new title. I was thinking of *When Your Mind's Full, Mind Less.*'

'You'll need a foreword explaining what a hero you are.' Toby went on to explain his adventures that day. Everyone in the room clapped. Flo was positively glowing with pride. The book that had lied, sighed and then smiled.

4: THE BOOKS THAT CRIED

The nights were drawing their margins ever closer to the day. The trees glowed their last sunset hurrahs as the mists gathered across the fields. The anticipation of warm fires and mulled wine held the bitter aftertaste of the cold dark nights to follow but Toby liked this time of year; the silver brightness of the wooded lanes, the mysterious light filtering through hazy air and the nutty smell of damp piles of leaves scattering before his feet. It was a time to gather harvests and thoughts. What had not prepared Toby were a locked library door and a notice from the council.

> *FINANCIAL CONSTRAINTS HAVE FORCED*
> *THE COUNCIL TO MAKE DIFFICULT*
> *DECISIONS TO PRESERVE OTHER SERVICES.*
> *WE ARE NO LONGER ABLE TO FUND*
> *THIS LIBRARY AND FROM THE*
> *31ST OCTOBER*
> *THIS LIBRARY WILL CLOSE.*
> *BY ORDER,*
>
> ### *CLLR JACOB CRUMBLE*

There was a time when Cllr Crumble would have used capital letters sparingly. Back then he was a thin slice of an accountant whose introverted shyness made him less assertive than an abacus. But he evolved to believe it was his right to make any pronouncement using only capitals. The cause of this transition was a steady rise through council strata. Like archaeological layers, these strata contained debris that stuck, and in Crumble's case all the detritus found a natural home. Whether you noticed the smell depended on how sensitive you were to the aroma of male oxen deposits. Multiple dining experiences at taxpayers' expense had created a dumpling that matched the heaviness felt in the pit of the stomachs of those who met him. His rounded face shone greasily around a bulbous nose overseeing thin, mean lips that silenced criticism. The fondness he showed his pet dog did not extend to his family or colleagues, although many suspected the dog was just biding its time. He hated books that were not ledgers. He could see no point in the wasteful use of time and letters. He had no patience for stories that dragged through multiple plots, subplots and sidelines and, despite his profession, he could not account for taste. He was clear that the only worthwhile story was a balanced audit, but with a profitable addendum for him and his pals, details of which were in a notebook filed under "S" for skimmed off the top. When Crumble said a project was interesting he meant 'with interest'.

'This is an interesting project,' Crumble mumbled to his long suffering clerk, Geoffrey Apple.

Geoffrey was a mirror image of what his boss had been, but Geoffrey's thinness hid a steely determination for fairness. His shyness and apparent stupidity were a shield against ignorance and bullying. He had never wanted to rise through the layers, having been distinctly unimpressed by their smell – Geoffrey could detect oxen deposits from a long way off. His quiet manner meant that Crumble had no idea how much he relied on Apple, but Apple knew exactly how much. In truth,

Apple & Crumble made a good team, but in this pie the Apple was biding its time.

'How is it interesting, sir?' asked Geoffrey in a way that invited a disdainful explanation one might give to a child in explaining why a ball was round.

Crumble prodded the map with a fat finger, 'This old library in the village here. Hardly visited, hardly used, draining money, ripe for development.'

'Development, sir?'

'Prime site for city folks to come and live.'

'But that will mean the village losing its library.'

'Of course, you buffoon, you have to make way for progress.' Crumble's method of making way for progress was to bulldoze through any opposition, preferably using real bulldozers.

'Progress with profit?' suggested Geoffrey.

'Are you just dense or have you learnt nothing?' Crumble's face was getting shinier and redder. 'Without profit there's no interest and without interest there's no profit.'

Geoffrey had noticed that Crumble rolled the 'pr' of profit in a way that made it sound like a delicate and rich chocolate desert. 'So, in a way, you're harvesting the library.'

'Surprisingly well put, Apple.'

'But you never planted the seeds.'

'What are you talking about, Apple?' He waved a pudgy hand. 'Go and annoy someone else. On the way, arrange for me to visit the library.'

Geoffrey scuttled away in a manner that implied servitude, but as soon as he was out of Crumble's sight he strode purposefully to his desk to pick up his coat, hat and umbrella. Geoffrey was going to visit a library. He liked libraries. They were refuges of knowledge, warmth and peace. They could be a little too reverential and he delighted in coughing or crinkling a sweet wrapper, daring other readers to join in. In truth, he had daydreams of dancing from desk to desk to the tune of Bohemian Rhapsody, leaping from Biography to Fiction in a single bound. Instead he would visit his sister Julie and take her for a spin around the living room carpet to whatever tune was playing on the radio. Julie's breathless giggles were the cue for Geoffrey's young niece and nephew to give their opinions. Six-year-old Becky would always score them 'Seven!', while three-year-old Thomas would just say 'You're silly' with a beaming smile. Today and, despite the rain, he was on a bus to a village.

Toby knocked but there was no answer and no light could be seen. He then noticed that someone had added a scrap of paper below the notice with an arrow and the word 'back'. He had no idea there was a back, although the presence of a front made a back a likely accompaniment. He went around the corner to a weed-lined path. This led to a door that had so many layers of paint that any flakes were a testimony to a remarkable variety of dark green shades. A faint light was visible through the rippled glass. Toby was about to knock when a shadow appeared behind the glass and the door opened to reveal Mary. Even when she was snoozing, Mary was always prim and proper, with an immaculate obligatory knot in her hair. She could look upright slumped over her desk. But today her hair was loose with strands escaping at different angles. She held a box tightly in bright yellow washing-up-gloved hands.

Mary's voice sighed with resignation, 'Thank you for coming, I've started to pack the books.'

'It must be a mistake, this can't be right.' Toby was struggling with the news. The thrill that teenagers feel with new experiences only worked if other parts of their lives were rigidly unchanged. Even the most experimental artist used boring everyday materials, although cutting animals in half and preserving them in formalin seemed to be stretching the point. The Library had become an important and stable part of Toby's life and he enjoyed his visits on the way back from school. He learnt more each evening than he did in a day at school, and the fact that the books helped with his homework was a bonus. His parents were very impressed by his scholarly application. The possibility of losing all this was very unsettling.

The room was eerily quiet but in the silence Toby could hear muffled sobs coming from the boxes. He could see the cardboard sides of some boxes shaking slightly. Fear and distress hung in the air like bonfire smoke on an autumn's evening. It was the creeping heaviness of the change that made it so ominous.

Toby was distraught. 'This can't be happening. They have no right!'

A book poked a spine over the edge of one of the boxes. Toby saw it was his sleuthing companion, Tabitha Crispy.

'Tabitha! What are you going to do, where are you going? Where am I going to go in the evenings? What about my homework?' Toby slumped down into the wicker chair which comforted him by sinking warmly around him, the armrest gently patting his hand.

'Mary is taking us to the archives in the Central library. It's unlikely anyone will find us there and we can distract the few that do. Perhaps Mary will be able to arrange a visit for you on occasions.' Tabitha's pages hunched over in dejection and she shook with cold trepidation.

Mary picked up Tabitha who settled into Mary's warm arms.

'But what will happen to your words? And what about the Library?'

A frown appeared in the corner of the room, followed by an angled nose, a manicured moustache, a down-set mouth framed by high cheekbones and a cleft chin. Toby had never seen the Library's face; it usually preferred to present a quizzical eyebrow, an unsettling staring eye, an assertive nose or a departing chin. Its manner was often superior, sceptical, cynical and critical but this time was different.

'I confess to being uncertain. I came with the stones but I do not know what will happen if the stones are separated. I cannot be certain if the words will continue to accumulate. It is very worrying.'

Toby had never heard the Library speak so many words, let alone admit it was worried. Until now it had not occurred to him that the Library might be destroyed.

It was hard enough hearing the books crying, but to lose the Library was frightening. Despite its haughty attitude, snide remarks and fondness for corners Toby found the Library a comforting presence. Its annoying habit of adding and subtracting corners had become a game which Toby sometimes won, probably because the Library let him win. Its sense of humour was not limited to creating new corners and corridors to confuse visitors. It liked to play tricks. Several times Toby had opened familiar doors to find a brick wall. This would be accompanied by a snigger disappearing up the corridor or an eye in one corner that looked at him and winked. Even when the Library stared at you from a dark corner, it felt oddly reassuring.

'We have to do something...' Toby was interrupted by a shadow and knock on the back door.

Strangers were usually met by Mary at the front desk. She was a good judge of character and knew whether they were going to browse briefly among the ordinary books or were simply in need of warmth and a chat. Some were allowed to meet the talking books and, of those that ventured through the Library's fluid corners, most refused to believe their eyes and ears and left with a determination to get a stiff drink and a long rest. A few like Toby, stayed and were entranced.

Still holding Tabitha in her arms, Mary looked up at the Library, 'Can we return to the front desk?'

'Of course.'

Mary held out a hand. 'Toby, follow me,' and she pulled Toby to the back door.

'I thought we were going to the front desk?'

'Wait.'

Toby watched the back door slide away from the two of them and become the solid front door. The walls widened until there was space for the desk and the shelves of ordinary books. Toby looked behind him and saw the usual bookshelves he had seen on his first visit. Mary tidied her hair, hid the yellow washing-up gloves in her desk and went to answer the door.

Geoffrey Apple shook his umbrella, removed his hat and extended a hand to Mary and stared.

'And you are?' asked Mary, staring back.

'S-sorry. Hallo, I'm Geoffrey.' Mary smiled and took his hand.

'I am Cllr Crumble's clerk.' Mary frowned and jerked back her hand. She could feel Tabitha squirming in her arms but held her firmly. She turned her back on

Geoffrey and placed Tabitha on the desk, putting a finger to her mouth in a silent 'Hush'.

To Mary's back, Geoffrey tried to explain, 'P-please, I am not here because of the library closure. No, sorry, I mean, I am here because of the closure...but not because I'm part of it, the closure I mean. Oh dear, I'm not explaining myself. Sorry.'

'You are sorry for yourself aren't you? It matches your wet coat and shoes,' observed Mary still with her back to Geoffrey. She pointed to Toby. 'This is Toby, a library member. I'm Mary, the librarian.'

'Good, it was you I wanted to see.'

Toby's anger spilled over. 'Have you come to gloat, enjoy your victory over the death of another library, rub salt into our wounds? You should be ashamed of yourself.'

Mary usually helped Toby redirect his anger so he could see its true source. This time she let it be, but then was surprised at Geoffrey's reply.

'Yes, ashamed. Ashamed of the decision and that I work for such an odious man.'

Mary turned to face Geoffrey and in her best 'Quiet!' librarian voice asked, 'Then why are you here?'

'I want to try to stop this, to keep the library open.'

This was not what they had expected. Mary's frown softened. 'Then you have a way of stopping this?'

Out of the corner of his eye Toby could see another eye appearing near the ceiling.

'I-I hadn't really thought that far ahead, sorry.'

The eye closed slowly and disappeared.

Mary knew how the eye felt. 'I had thought you might be able to help.'

From the desk behind Mary, Tabitha poked a page corner over the top and whispered to Mary's back 'Don't know what made you think Crumble's browbeaten clerk was going to help.'

Geoffrey straightened up and seemed more solid in the gloom. He looked at Mary and explained, 'I am not browbeaten. My brow has never succumbed to Crumble or his machinations. My bumbling demeanour suits Crumble and protects my job, but he does *not* have my soul.'

'At least he has a soul,' chipped in Tabitha.

Geoffrey looked behind Mary, 'Who said that?'

'You did,' lied Mary, waving her hand at Tabitha. 'Is there any way you can help?'

Geoffrey's frown was as much over the source of the voice behind Mary as to his reply. 'There might be a way. I was thinking that we could...'

A loud knocking on the front door interrupted Geoffrey, accompanied by Crumble's familiar rant, 'Let me in, you buffoons. I demand to see this dilapidated ruin!'

Mary 'shooshed' everyone, determined to leave him out in the wet and cold, but the Library had other ideas. The front door swung open with an ominous creak that would have honoured the best horror film. Toby and Mary had always known the door to be well oiled and silent. The Library was up to something.

'Good! You're packing. I expect you all out by Saturday,' said Crumble, as Geoffrey stepped out of the shadows. 'Apple! What are you doing here?'

Crumble was surprised that Apple seemed taller and more substantial than this morning. He was even more surprised by his reply.

'I intend to stop you closing and demolishing this library.'

Crumble's face became red and shiny. 'Don't act the fool, Apple. The decision is made. Anyone who gets in my way will regret they were ever born and that includes you, Apple.'

Crumble strode over to the desk and picked up Tabitha. 'I am going to make sure that you and this dingy derelict warehouse of useless books disappears forever.'

Mary, Toby and Geoffrey's memories of the next few seconds were a series of detailed images that rushed by like a Victorian zoetrope. Mary saw Tabitha open up in Crumble's hands but was too late to stop her snapping down on Crumble's fingers with a crunch that hurt as much to hear as to feel. Crumble threw Tabitha on the desk in shock. He spotted an old fire axe on the wall and reached for the handle. Crumble raised the axe to strike Tabitha. But before he could act, the Library *folded*.

Its silence was more menacing than the way the corner wrapped around Crumble, gripping his arm. In seconds his body had disappeared, leaving his red nose and a bulging eye filled with horror. His shout was cut short, as he sank further into the cavity. After a few moments the wall unfolded and returned to a normal empty cranny, complete with cobwebs and surprised spiders.

'What have you done with him?' shouted Geoffrey.

A smug smile appeared in the corner. *'Do not worry, he is safe. I have simply shown him the back door. Shame he tripped over the doorstep, I've been meaning to fix that for a while....'*

Geoffrey stood with his mouth open, but Mary and Toby just laughed.

Outside, Crumble's nose was squashed against the pavement, his nostrils expanding and contacting as he struggled to catch his breath. He lifted his head, leaving a splatter of blood to blur into the rain. He was confused, but as he got up he became angry. He staggered back to his office, each step stiffening with determined revenge.

5: THE BOOKS THAT HIDE

Geoffrey was not sure whether to keep his mouth open in silence, or open it to speak, or run. His indecision was broken by Toby who whispered 'Well done!' to Tabitha on the desk.

'Thank you,' said a stunned Geoffrey, unsure why he wasn't running.

Tabitha curled a page into a smile as Mary gently picked her up.

Mary pointed in the direction of the talking books. 'Toby, I think Geoffrey could do with a sit down, a cup of tea and an explanation.'

The journey was surprisingly free of corners. Either the Library was having a day off or it had warmed to

Geoffrey. The newcomer sank gratefully into the wicker chair which had wisely decided that patting his hand might be a bit much for him at the moment. Toby went behind the shelves to make tea. He was faced with two books fighting and flapping their pages at each other in clouds of flour, scattering an asteroid shower of raisins on a sunny butter surface that glistened with spilt sugar and cream. The completed scones sat in the midst of the mess, lonely outcrops on a storm-lashed surface.

       'The cream always goes on top of the jam!'

       'Rubbish! The jam goes on top of the cream.'

       'And you didn't get proper Cornish cream,
           did you?'

       'Better than the cheap supermarket gloop
           you got last time.'

       'Amateur!'

       'Dilettante!'

Cordon 'Blue' Fancy and Gamey Pullover were rival chefs. They had accumulated their recipes from a multitude of celebrity chef cookery books but it did not take long for everyone in the Library to realise that their words had arrived with egos attached and intact. Cordon and Gamey's tempers had not been helped by being misclassified in Fashion, and their race to the Cookery section had been accompanied by tantrums, clattering pans, burnt fingers and flying polenta chips. They were both always on the boil but this hid a mutual respect for each other. In truth, they were a match made in oven.

'Stop it!' whispered Toby. 'We've got a visitor.'

Cordon and Gamey peeked around the shelf, leaving a trail of flour and raisins. Geoffrey was too busy looking at his feet to notice, still trying to make sense of what he had seen.

Cordon looked shamefaced. 'How were we supposed to know? We were busy getting a farewell tea together. It's been a trying time.'

'I understand. But, if you look after this visitor he may be able to help us stop the Library being closed.' explained Toby.

'Ah!' Gamey looked questioningly at Cordon. 'Can we help?' Cordon nodded.

'Cups of tea would be good. With scones. Half with the cream on top, half with jam on top. OK?'

The chefs both nodded and turned to clear up and get started.

Toby pulled up a stool in front of Geoffrey. 'I need to explain something.'

'What, that I'm hallucinating and going mad?'

'You're not seeing things,' reassured Toby.

'I saw Crumble being swallowed by a wall!' – a statement that would usually make it clear the speaker was having difficulties.

'I saw that too. It's fairly normal around here.'

'But what happened to Crumble? Is he dead? Is this place dangerous?' Geoffrey's eyes had widened in panic.

'No, no,' replied Toby calmly, 'If the Library says he's safe, then he's safe.'

'I thought that voice was in my head!'

'No, that was real too. This is a strange but wonderful place. Perhaps Mary could explain?'

Toby stood up as Mary came in carrying a book. Mary looked at Geoffrey and said softly, 'What you've seen and heard is just part of the wonder. Are you ready to learn more?'

The gentleness of her voice made Geoffrey look up and whisper 'Yes.'

Mary slowly handed Geoffrey the book. 'This is Tabitha. She has something to tell you.'

Geoffrey stood up and reached out with trembling hands. In the midst of this strangeness, for some reason, he felt trusted. He placed the book on the stool in front of him, unsure what to do. He started to reach out when the book slowly opened and sat up. Geoffrey fell back into the chair, but instead of panic, he smiled with curiosity.

'Hello Geoffrey, I'm Tabitha.'

Geoffrey's surprise was that he wasn't surprised, though his jaw disagreed by dropping.

'You can close your mouth now,' said Tabitha.

Geoffrey closed his mouth and grinned. 'I suppose I was expecting a deep philosophical gem of wisdom that would give immediate meaning to my life.'

Tabitha's pages shook with giggles. 'Sorry to disappoint you. I had assumed you'd had enough life-changing experiences for today. But if you want more...'

'No!' Geoffrey held up his hand. 'Thank you for the kind offer but after a very strange day, meeting you takes the biscuit.'

Cordon and Gamey knew a cue when they heard one.

'Biscuits! Name your preference.'

'We can make arrowroot, amaretti, biscotti, bannock, bourbon....'

'Brandy snap, caramel, chocolate, crackers, crispbread....'

'Digestive, flapjack, florentine, garbaldi, ginger....'

'Macaroon, oatcake, petit four, pretzel, rich
tea, shortbread....'

'Umm....wafer.'

'And umm....water biscuit.'

Mary interrupted, 'Thank you, boys, that's wonderful. But did I hear you've just made some scones. They would be perfect.'

Cordon and Gamey disappeared, still arguing.

'You forgot rusks.'

'And you forgot drop biscuits.'

Geoffrey was fascinated by the cookery tutorial and looked at Tabitha. 'So, you aren't the only book who can talk!'

He was answered by a chorus of voices from the boxes and the shelves echoed with hellos and words of welcome.

'What do you think?' asked Mary.

Geoffrey stood up, 'This is wonderful! Marvellous!' Then he remembered and clenched his fists. 'We have to stop Crumble.'

Toby looked at Mary and then the ceiling. 'We're going to need some help.'

An eye appeared in one corner.

'I am happy to help. I hope you approved of my showing Cllr Crumble the door, although I doubt that my approach will have helped his mood.'

Geoffrey had to sit down again. This was only the second time in his life that a huge face had appeared in the corner of a room, and twice in a day was a bit much, but he managed to agree. 'I suspect it will have made him seethingly irritated. He'll be plotting his revenge.'

Mary put on her most organised demeanour. 'Right, let's start planning, but first some tea and scones.'

At the council offices Crumble was on the phone.

'I want you down there first thing tomorrow morning. Bring in whatever and whoever you need. I want it done by the evening. Yes, I know it's a Saturday. No, whatever it costs. Yes, you have free rein. Alright, cash up front. Yes, you'll get it this evening.'

On the other end of the phone Jeff was rubbing his chin with cement-stained puzzlement. He had worked for Crumble before but there was always some problem such as people still living in houses earmarked for demolition. He had distrusted Crumble from the start and saw him as a greasy blob on the make. Jeff was no lightweight himself but he knew that his pounds were honestly accumulated. Crumble seemed too keen to see good buildings disappear, usually for profitable and expensive housing. Despite being an accountant, Crumble had no concept of affordable housing. Jeff had given his excuses in recent years, but jobs were going to be scarce this coming winter and this job was being paid up front, although his suspicions were not allayed by being handed cash in a deserted car park.

In the Library, more had joined the group and the tea and scones had gone down well, much to the satisfaction of the chefs. Tabitha had explained how their rejected words accumulated in this library and why their names and titles varied from the originals. Geoffrey was much more diplomatic than Toby at hiding his amusement at Carl Chicken's *A Twist of Olive* but couldn't resist asking Carl if he would like a dry martini. Tabitha curled over her pages and shook with silent giggles, but Toby and Mary had to go behind the shelves to hide their laughter with coughs and sneezes. Fortunately Carl predated Martinis and seemed to take no notice. Geoffrey was impressed by Sir Donald Coil. He was tempted to ask if his *Gairloch Homes* contained any advice on house prices, but it was difficult to make a joke at the expense of someone who looked at you with such a fierce, forensic glare. He saw through the Bronty sisters' lace and charm and suspected that if he reached out to them without permission he would lose his fingers, probably one at a time. Ilack Azimuth and Luckless Atoms kept coming up with suggestions that wouldn't be invented for centuries, if ever.

Theo Toaster was a bundle of enthusiasm but had a tendency to invent deviously lethal traps to catch any intruders. The others persuaded him that simpler measures would be adequate without any need for death or destruction, so he settled into planning mode with a series of grunts and humphs. Jarr Talkin kept poking his pipe up in the air and saying that what they needed was a wizard. Everyone else assumed he was in one of his adventures in muddled soil or whatever it was called, until they realised his pipe was pointing up at the corner of the room where a face waited patiently.

'My apologies,' said Mary, 'we have not asked for your thoughts.'

'Thank you. Perhaps we could consider the worst scenario and prepare for that.'

Toby spread out his arms. 'How do you prepare for bulldozers and men with pick axes?'

Geoffrey had the answer to that. 'Actually, it's simple. We make it clear the building is still occupied.'

'And if that doesn't work?'

'Then we will need to be imaginative.'

'Toby, it's getting late and your parents will be wondering where you are. We can make the final preparations tonight,' said Mary and seeing Toby's concern added, 'We'll be fine. Come back in the morning.'

Toby looked towards the chefs, 'At least you'll have plenty of biscuits.' On cue, came the clattering of baking tins going into the oven.

The next morning, Toby got up early, had some toast and told his parents he was going to the library. His father looked over his paper and said casually, 'Don't bother. When I went to get the paper they were putting up boarding and getting a bulldozer off a lorry. Shame, it's the only library around for miles.'

Toby dropped his toast and ran out, grabbing his coat and gloves. As he turned the corner he saw his father was right. Grey boarding now covered the fencing around the library except for an opening into which a large yellow bulldozer was churning its rattling, fume-laden way towards the building.

'Stop!' shouted Toby, running towards the front door.

A large cement-lined hand halted Toby in his tracks. 'And where do you think you're going, sonny boy?'

Toby looked into a round face topped by a bright yellow hard hat, matched with an extra large yellow fluorescent high visibility jacket. Jeff looked like a sumo wrestler who was moonlighting as a school crossing patrol officer. His face was trying to be stern but the laugh lines around his eyes told a different story.

'I'm going to the library to do some homework,' explained Toby.

'Not today or any other day for that matter. We're here to take it down.'

'You can't, there are people in there!'

In Jeff's early dealings with Crumble he had ignored such claims as attempts to delay the inevitable, until he spotted an elderly face at an upper window just as he was about to demolish a house. He had stopped dealing with Crumble soon after. Was history repeating itself?

Jeff thought it wise to check, 'How do you know?'

'Because they told me last night that they would be staying put.'

Jeff sighed. 'OK, let's see shall we? But if you're wrong....'

'I'm not,' said Toby with confidence.

Jeff banged on the door. 'Is there anyone in there?'

'Yes!' came the reply.

Jeff was beginning to regret ever agreeing to this job, but not to having been paid up front. 'Who's there?'

'I'm Mary, the librarian.'

'And I'm Geoffrey Apple, Cllr Crumble's clerk. We're not moving from here.' This was followed by shouts of 'Quite right!', 'Absolutely not, you cad!', 'Nikogda!', 'We have lasers!' and 'There'll be no biscuits for you, ever.'

Jeff stood back from the door, 'How many are in there?'

Mary replied, 'Two of us at the door but lots behind us.'

Geoffrey shouted, 'Dozens more.'

'I knew it!' exclaimed Jeff and got on his phone to Crumble. 'Yep, the librarian and your clerk. No, the doors are locked and solid. No, I will not use the bulldozer.' He held the phone from his ear while Crumble shouted and swore. Once there was a silent gap Jeff interrupted, 'You do know there are dozens in there on a protest? This is not going to look good in the papers. In fact, here's the lady from the *Echo* now. Sorry, have to do a media interview.'

Amelia knew Jeff as a solid and honest citizen. 'Hello Jeff. Can't believe they're closing down another library. I like this old building. Who approved this?'

'Guess who?' said Jeff.

'Crumble,' they both said together.

'What's stopped you?'

Jeff explained, 'People have locked themselves in there protesting at the closure. Sounds like lots of people. Dozens they claim.'

Amelia brightened up. 'Ooo, good. Can I go and speak to them?'

'Of course, I'm not doing anything while people are in there.'

Amelia went up to the door and knocked quietly. 'I'm Amelia Brentworth from the *Echo*. Could I come in? I'd like to do a piece on your situation.'

There was much whispering from behind the door. Jeff was right, it sounded like lots of whispers.

Mary replied through the door, 'What do you think of libraries, Amelia?'

'I used to come to this library all the time as a child. Had a nice warm feel about it. Now I have to use the Central library with all its IT links, but it's not the same.'

'Toby, are you out there?' asked Mary.

'Yes. I think she could help. Jeff is a good bloke; he won't do anything while you're all in there.'

The locks were turned and the doors opened smoothly, without a sound. It took a while for Amelia to adjust her eyes, but the cosy feel took her straight back to a shy 10-year old, excited at finding her next instalment. She used to wander the cathedral aisles lined with knowledge, excitement and anticipation. She had found the wicker chair many times and would sit reading her latest borrowed book, safe in its creaking comfort. Surrounded by words, she would have conversations. At home she did this in front of the mirror, hands on hips using her mum's facial expressions, shoes and lipstick. Those were one sided but her conversations in the library were two, three or four sided and felt exciting, a secret adventure she shared with no-one. As the years went by Amelia had found it harder to remember the details of those discussions, but their memory had influenced her life in ways she could not imagine.

The doors closed and Mary, Geoffrey and Toby introduced themselves.

Amelia was puzzled. 'I thought there was a crowd in here.'

'In a way there is,' said Mary. Toby and Geoffrey shook their heads but Mary ignored them and continued. 'Would you like to sit in the wicker chair again?'

'Is it still here? Yes!' said Amelia, feeling the excited trepidation of a 10-year old.

'There are some old friends there who would like to say hello,' said Mary.

Amelia responded with an odd, puzzled look, but she knew where to go and the Library obliged. She stopped behind the wicker chair and stroked its back, her fingers trembling slightly. Hesitantly she sat down, the chair trying to make her feel at ease with soothing creaks. A familiar voice spoke to her.

'Hello Amelia, it's good to see you again,' said Merrily Bronty.

Amelia sat bolt upright and ran out of the room.

Mary was surprised to see Merrily returning on her own. 'Where's Amelia?'

'I do not know. She became very frightened when I spoke to her and ran out.'

'What frightened her?' asked Mary.

'I think I know, but I need to speak to her now, alone. Library, do you know where she is?'

'She is in the empty section next to the old wooden shelves.'

Merrily found Amelia on the floor holding a candle whose reflection danced on her tears.

'Stay away!' whispered Amelia in a voice strangled with anxiety. 'I thought coming back here would help, but it's worse.'

'Why is it worse? You used to enjoy our conversations.' Merrily reached out a page.

Amelia shrank away from the offered page, clutching her candle. 'I was TEN! You're allowed to have imaginary conversations, its expected, part of growing up. But as I got older I realised the voices were in my head. I'd managed to lock that fear away but now I'm here and the voices are back. It means I'm sick and my daughter will probably end up like me. But the voices are only here. That's why Crumble has to get rid of this place.'

'Amelia no! You don't understand, our talks were real, cherished.'

'They won't be any more.' With a shaking hand she held her candle to some scrap of paper on the desiccated wooden shelf which caught fire with a sudden 'whomp'.

'Now I can get peace.'

6: THE BOOKS THAT GUIDE

The dry wooden shelves sucked up the flames, sending up a black cloud of dust and smoke that rolled across the ceiling and started to sink to the floor. Amelia shrank away from the flames and smoke. Her wide eyes oscillated between both, trying to ignore the book approaching her. Amelia dropped onto the floor in fear.

'Amelia! We have to get out now,' shouted Merrily, reaching across to try to pull Amelia's hand. Amelia hit out and knocked Merrily into the flames. Merrily shrieked and fell onto the floor, pages smouldering. She groaned with pain but reached out once more, pleading, 'Please!'

Amelia kicked Merrily across the floor and slapped her hands around her ears.

'Leave me alone! I've lived with the memory of these voices all my life and I want them gone.'

As a 10-year old, Amelia's conversations had been enjoyable make-believe fun. They had felt real but over time it had become a fear that the voices could return at anytime. She had coped by seeking out facts through journalism which had filled her time and mind. That was until she spotted her 6-year-old daughter Callie standing in front of the mirror, hand on hip, having an animated conversation. All the fears of her library voices came flooding back and she had been determined to ensure Callie was never exposed to them. When Crumble had called her she quickly realised he was trying to forestall bad publicity from the library closure. She was always wary of his machinations but the memories of the library were too strong to resist. Facing your fears was easy to say but hard to do, and she had not been sure what she would find. Now she knew.

She was on her own and it was getting hotter by the second. All she could see around her were walls dancing with flames. Crawling to where the smoke was higher she spotted a window. Standing up she could see Crumble outside. Banging on the window's metal bars she shouted, 'Help! I'm trapped!' Crumble saw her, nodded and, with a faint smile, turned around and walked away, ignoring her shouts and the flickering flames. He stopped at the corner to speak to someone, probably Jeff, but to her dismay Crumble waved his hand in a 'Nothing there' gesture and walked out of sight. Her hate for that man was only matched by her hate of herself. Amelia hit the wall with frustration. How could she think she could return here and exorcise her fears? On the contrary, she must be deteriorating – she had only heard voices as a child but now she was seeing talking books.

Theo had been busy. Tea from a teapot instead of a samovar was not his, well, cup of tea, let alone bicarbonate-tasting scones and the frivolous arguments over the correct order of scones, cream and jam. This was war and preparation was essential. He had spent his time gathering a host of items, positioning them at key points and making plans with the Library. He was in his element and this was his moment. He raced along the shelves towards the smoke and flames, dropping lower until he was sliding across the floor. He grabbed two items he had placed there overnight. The heat was getting stronger. He had discarded his dust cover and his leather cover was going to give him some protection, although his constant engineering and tinkering had stained the cover with oil which was not the best protection against fire. It was bad enough to feel his title page getting warm but the idea that his frontispiece might come to harm was not a pleasant thought. He could see very little now and the flames were close enough to risk igniting his oil-soaked cover. He pulled out the two objects from under his pages and got to work.

Amelia was coughing, crawling and scratching a way out, cursing that creep Crumble. But as she realised her reality, revenge was replaced by regret. The siren call to face her voices was a selfish action that could now cost her life and her daughter Callie. It was at that moment that her world changed. The black smoke was replaced by a thick white cloud and the roaring flames were overcome by a loud, continuous hissing and spluttering. Something gripped her hand and pulled her into breathable air. On the floor she noticed a line of lights leading away from the smoke.

'*Follow me,*' said a deep voice.

She hesitated. The library voices had haunted her all her life and here was another one.

A different voice begged her, 'Please, rebenok. Child, Amelia, I'm here to help, not hurt.'

In the haze she could see a shape ahead and followed on her hands and knees. Her eyes were streaming from the smoke and fear. Through her tears the walls seemed to blur and change shape. The floor became cooler and the air clearer. Eventually she knew she was safe and lay on the floor coughing and sobbing in relief. Mary knelt down and helped Amelia sit up. What faced Amelia made her want to return to the floor. Next to Toby and Geoffrey were a multitude of books, each busy moving around the library and, most disconcerting of all, *talking*.

She looked pleadingly at Mary who took Amelia's head in her hands and looked into her eyes. 'Yes, they are real, we can all see and hear them. In fact, it was Theo who saved your life. That and his sensible idea of setting up extra fire extinguishers throughout the Library. We all owe him a great thanks.'

Theo peeped around Mary, his cover steaming but fortunately not burning. He shrugged his pages. 'It seemed sensible. Good to see you safe, rebenok.'

Trembling with incredulous emotion, Amelia managed a tremulous 'Thank you' and then remembered kicking a book into the flames. 'But I think I may have hurt one of you, or worse.' She held her head in her hands, sobbing.

Merrily limped out from behind Toby, her cover and pages singed and blackened, 'Amelia, I am safe – sore, but safe.'

'I'm so sorry, but your voice was so frightening. I remembered our conversations but I had convinced myself they were all in my head. I don't know how to thank you.'

A cough came from ceiling.

'We all played our part. I quite liked the emergency lights in the floor. I wanted to have exit signs front, middle and rear, but Theo thought that was going too far.'

A humph came from Theo. 'We're a library. With foundations. Not an airplane.'

'Still, I liked the idea.'

Mary interrupted, 'All the ideas were good and they worked. But Crumble and Jeff are still outside and we need to plan our next steps.'

Amelia stood up, clenching her fists. 'Crumble saw me at the window. He walked away! He was prepared to let me burn! He's not going to get away with this.'

Together they sat down to plan, to the background accompaniment of more scones and biscuits being cooked.

Crumble had walked round from the back of the Library. 'Nothing there, we'll just have to wait for them to come out. I don't think they'll be long.'

Jeff looked at Crumble, then at the flickering glow at the side of the library. 'What have you done?'

Crumble shrugged and sat on a wall. It was irrelevant how the fire had started; what mattered was that the library would be his now. As he looked up, the flames were beginning to take hold and creep under the roof tiles. All that dry, tedious monotony made good fuel and the flames would do their job faster and, more importantly, cheaper, than that jelly, Jeff.

Jeff started towards the door. Crumble pulled him back, mumbling, 'Any minute now.'

Sure enough, the front door opened and out came the prim librarian and that traitor Apple, both carrying boxes full of useless books. Crumble turned and walked away, his job done. What he failed to see was Amelia following behind clutching two books and boring her eyes into Crumble's cowardly back. He did not see Mary and Geoffrey holding Jeff back and reassuring him that no-one else was in the building.

The Library fire continued to devour the roof timbers and flames soared into the sky accompanied by the sound of crashing tiles, timbers and walls. The speed of the fire was remarkable and Jeff directed them all to safety behind the grey hoarding. By the time blue lights were flickering on the other side of the village the Library had collapsed and no fire could be seen, not even a glowing ember.

Jeff was stunned by the disaster and gently laid a hand on Mary's arm. 'I'm so sorry. I know what it meant to you. It was a lovely building.'

'It still is,' said Mary facing the Library.

Jeff turned around to find the Library was unchanged, intact, with not a singe or burn in sight. 'How did you manage that?'

Mary and Geoffrey looked blank but Toby jumped in with an explanation. 'It's amazing what you can do with special effects, lighting, projected images, fireworks, sound effects and some smoke.' None of them was going to explain how the Library had just played the performance of its life.

'Well, it fooled me and certainly fooled Crumble. I can't wait to tell him.'

'Could you wait until morning?' asked Amelia. 'I'd like to see his reaction in person.'

Geoffrey added, 'And I have something that will interest your readers.'

In the council offices the next morning, Crumble was rocking back and forth on his leather padded, ergonomically designed office chair with five preset positions, lumbar support and unique patented 'Posterior-Fit' feature. It had been a profitable day's work. Now the *Echo* wanted to see him, no doubt to talk about his development plans for the site, but he blanched as Amelia walked in.

'Surprised to see me, Crumble? Last time I saw you I was about to burn to death behind a locked window. You actually smiled as you walked away.'

'N-n-no, you're mistaken, I never saw you,' stumbled Crumble.

'You were always a bad liar.' She was interrupted by Crumble's mobile phone ringing. It was Jeff, on cue.

'What do you mean, it's still there? I saw it burn down! I heard it crash! You're lying to me, you toad.' Crumble cut him off, but his phone rang again. This time Jeff sent a video link. Amelia heard Jeff say, 'You need to see this.' Crumble watched in silence, flopping down into his posterior fitted chair.

Crumble saw Amelia smile and reacted. 'Don't be smug with me! If I've been tricked it makes no difference. That library is still coming down. Now get out. I have developers to meet.'

'Before doing that you might like to read this morning's *Echo*,' said Amelia, throwing a copy on his desk with the headline *Crook Crumble crumbles*.

Crumble's face became an angry beetroot. 'This is slander! You come in here with false accusations and fake news. You have no right to call yourself a journalist. I'll make sure you don't work on the *Echo* or any other paper. How dare you print such lies. You have no proof!'

Geoffrey walked in. 'I think you'll find that this is all the proof we need.' He held up a rather tattered notebook. 'Filed under "S" I believe. It contains some very interesting accounting to which you and some friends are key beneficiaries. There are some colleagues from the local constabulary who are waiting for you in the office.'

All Crumble could say was, 'Apple....'

Back in the Library, Cordon and Gamey were hidden behind piles of scones and biscuits. The jam/cream battle had been resolved by relinquishing the decision to the consumer who didn't seem to mind either way. Mary and Geoffrey sat between the shelves sharing scones, books and looks. Toby was listening to Theo tell his tales of engineering and fire-fighting, with typically modest tales of daring-do from the Library. And in the wicker chair sat Amelia with Callie on her lap. Callie was deep in an animated conversation with Merrily and Theo.

Amelia smiled at the books that had been her guide.

7: THE BOOK INSIDE

Betty Blanchett was in little doubt that in the war against time the years were winning. Ninety-eight years had a habit of ambushing you in imaginative ways. What had started as an occasional grunt on getting out of a chair had become a sofa-esque pirouette to the vertical, accompanied by musical wind whose embarrassment had lessened as the deafness had worsened. Like the weekend's best goal the sofa adventure was in slow motion and replayed several times until the standing position was reached. Protocol then demanded striking out across the floor while negotiating coffee tables and rugs that were scheming to bump your shins or trip you up. Normal life now required walking aids that were too bulky to be convenient and hearing aids that were too small to be useful. The entrance requirement for famous heroes is often a solo crossing of inhospitable terrain or sea, preferably while losing parts of your anatomy. Few acknowledged that getting across the living room floor could be heroic for some. And yet, this was a woman who at ninety-six thought *The Full Monty* was boring because the last scene was filmed from behind – Betty's mind was having no difficulty keeping well ahead of her body.

Betty went through to open up for business. She unlocked the door, turned the ageing sign to 'open' and looked back into the memories of her bookshop. She had arrived from France on VE day to join her husband. He had been in the Free French Army and had joined the British Army as the war drew to a close. She had started in the bookshop to help an elderly owner who could no longer move books and see customers. She rapidly learnt English and helped him stock up with French books to serve the growing French community. When the owner died she had been stunned to find he had left her the bookshop in his will. The bookshop soon became a hub for Anglo-French relations, filled with *Gitanes* smoke, the smell of *Pastis* and the sound of Edith Piaf. Now it was a quiet second-hand bookshop filled with dust, the smell of warm toast and the sound of BBC News.

Amelia had been returning from the library with her daughter Callie when she saw Betty opening the bookshop. Callie pulled her towards the faded door.

'Look, Mummy, another library! Let's go in!'

Amelia explained, 'It's a bookshop, where you buy books to keep, instead of borrowing them and returning them to the library.'

Callie was imagining having a permanent talking friend to gossip with at home. 'I want to keep some books.' She was through the door before Amelia could stop her. The bell above the door tinkled a welcome, making Callie giggle.

Betty turned around at the sounds. 'Welcome, young lady. And you too, Madame.' This was said with a French accent that had hardly lessened since VE day.

'My daughter wanted to see your shop; she thought it was a library.'

'Well, in a way, that is what it has become. Few people come in here to buy books these days and I cannot resist refusing those who want to borrow a book.'

'I told you it was a library,' admonished Callie in her usual hands-on-hip stance when she was being stern. 'Where are the talking books?'

Betty frowned with a polite smile and looked at Amelia. 'And what do you know about talking books, my dear?'

'Oh, she means the ones that make noises that match the pictures,' said Amelia, trying to pull Callie back to the door.

Callie was having none of it. 'Not those books, they're for babies! I mean the ones we talk to at the other library.'

Amelia was trying to think how to explain a child's overactive imagination when Betty interrupted her thoughts.

'Ah! Do you know Mary the *bibliothécaire*?' Amelia nodded. Betty continued, 'She lets me borrow some special books sometimes... if they want a trip out of the library.' She gave Amelia a knowing smile.

'We don't want to put you to any trouble.'

'*Pas du tout.* No problem. I have a few in the back if you would like to follow me.'

Betty took them into her lounge at the back of the shop, switched off the radio and went to the small kitchen. 'Would you like some tea and scones?'

'Did Cordon and Gamey make them?' asked Callie.

'I hope you don't mind, but I made these. Are those two still arguing whether the cream or the jam goes on top?' said Betty.

Amelia was reassured that Betty knew the Library's inhabitants. 'They're still at it, but it doesn't seem to slow up the number of cakes they make. They are really the best of *patisserie* friends.'

Callie shrugged, trying to see where she kept her special books.

Betty laughed at the shared friendship and went to a shelf in the corner where four books were sitting politely. She held out her hand to Callie. 'Would you like to meet my friends?' Callie nodded excitedly. Four pairs of eyes swivelled in her direction. Betty pulled up a Callie-sized wicker chair and a small table for the four books. In moments Callie and the books were chatting like best friends.

'Who are they?' asked Amelia quietly.

'Meet Ronald Dull of *Charlie and the Sprocket Factory.* You and Callie will know Dahl's wonderful books. Ronald's book is more about gears and pulleys than confectionary, which explains why he's filed under Manufacturing, but he remains a wonderful storyteller.' Ronald waved a cheery page.

'Peas Louis' *The Lie-in, the Stitch and the Bathrobe* has echoes of the Narnia stories but with less religion and more fashion. He is a firm believer in roughage and has a preference for dressing in duvets on a cold day.' Betty and Amelia had broad grins as Peas shook a well-manicured page at them.

'As for Gnarl,' Betty continued, 'you'll know his brother author, Carl Chickens. Gnarl Thickens has not really improved on the name and his *A Trail of Committees* – yes, he's derived from *A Tale of Two Cities* – was not helped by being filed under Management.' Gnarl threw a crumpled agenda at them accompanied by a grin.

'What about the last one in fatigues and safety boots?'

'Ah! That's Miss Nomer. Her book *The Myriad* is a bit of a mystery, as was the ancient Greek author, Homer. She decided the way was open for some strong characterisation as a vegan urban poet.'

Miss Nomer stuck out a boot and a thumbs-up in welcome.

'Wasn't Homer a man?' whispered Amelia.

'That's not the sort of detail that would bother Miss Nomer,' explained Betty.

Amelia and Betty eavesdropped on the conversation. Callie was in full flow.

'The Library nearly burnt down and my mummy was caught in the fire but she was saved by the books, especially Uncle Theo. He's funny.'

Ronald had never thought of Theo as funny but was proud that his friend had been the hero. He looked at Amelia. 'So what happened?'

Amelia decided that it might not help to admit that she was an arsonist, but made a resolution to explain the truth to Callie when she was older. 'I'll let Callie tell the story.'

Callie rushed on, 'And then the clever Library did some tricks to make it look like it was crashing down. Boom!' Callie emphasised the drama with outstretched hands and crunching sounds. 'The fat man from the council went away, he thought he'd won. But he was wrong! Mummy and Geoffrey made sure of that by getting him arrested.' She clapped her hands shut like the closing door of a jail.

'Who's Geoffrey?' asked Gnarl.

'Sorry,' explained Betty, 'I've been too busy to take the books back. It seems as if we've missed out on the drama, fun and gossip.' Amelia realised the four books had been in the bookshop for a while, but was not convinced by Betty's excuse that she was busy. Her shop looked as if it hadn't seen business for a long while. Her thoughts were interrupted by Callie putting her hand up and jumping up and down.

'I know who he is, I do. I know. Shall I tell them?' Callie looked as if she would burst with the knowledge. She had recently discovered gossip was a gold-plated bargaining chip, especially if it embarrassed her mother. She had also begun to realise that gossip could hurt, but that being given permission to reveal secrets was delicious.

'Alright Callie, would you like to tell us?' said Amelia, her grin matching the others in the room.

Callie was still fidgeting with excitement. 'Well, Geoffrey Apple was Cllr Crumble's clerk....'

'Apple - Crumble, a delicious combination,' noted Miss Nomer.'

'Except that Geoffrey hates Crumble and loves the Library,' explained Callie.

Peas piped up, 'Never would have happened if I had been there to advise on their diet.'

'The world's problems are not all solved by roughage, Peas,' retorted Miss Nomer.

Ronald pondered for a moment. 'But if Archimedes could think of a lever long enough to move the world, perhaps enough roughage could clear the largest pile of ....'

'Thank you Ronald,' interrupted Betty, 'we shall leave you with that thought and I have no doubt it will appear in one of your future stories.'

'Mmm. I may call it *Peas and the World's Biggest Stool.*'

'Not funny,' said Peas.

'Perhaps we should evacuate the room now,' added Amelia with a very serious expression.

'You're not helping,' grunted Peas.

Amelia and Callie dropped into the bookshop whenever they could. Callie loved listening to Ronald's stories, including his latest, which Callie explained to Amelia was about eating your greens on a very large chair. Peas and Miss Nomer would have long arguments over suitable fashion, although Callie could not understand why Miss Nomer was so against something called Loo Button shoes. Most surprising was Gnarl whose gruff demeanour hid an infinite patience in listening to Callie, no matter what her stories, grumbles or flights of fancy. Amelia admired his calm listening and wished she had the same gift. Betty's reluctance to take the books back to the Library was becoming understandable. Betty had read all the books in her shop, many several times. Company was infrequent and these four books were wonderful companions. Despite this, Amelia wondered if the books might want to return to the Library and intended to ask them at the next visit.

That next visit was delayed by Amelia's work and some birthday parties for Callie's friends. Callie had never enjoyed parties. They just seemed noisy events of overdressed, extrovert children, unpleasant food and parents, followed by fullness and nausea. Amelia often stayed during the parties in case Callie needed reassurance or rescue. After one party with entertainers that insisted everyone join in, Callie needed rescuing and wanted to go to the bookshop. They arrived late afternoon and found the door locked. Callie knocked on the glass, rattling the bell inside. After a while a pale-looking Betty saw Callie and came to unlock the door.

'Hello Callie, Amelia. Today's not a good day, perhaps you could come back tomorrow,' implored Betty, evidently exhausted.

'I need to come in!' pleaded Callie. From an early age Callie had used 'need' when she wanted something badly and Amelia has lost count how many times she had told her 'Just because you *want* something doesn't mean you *need* it.'

Amelia put her hand on Betty's arm. 'Tell me what's wrong. Perhaps we can help?'

Betty slowly opened the door but locked it behind them. The bookshop looked unchanged except that, unusually, the four books were on the desk, each looking in different directions. Callie was unusually quiet and kept close to Amelia as they followed Betty into the lounge behind the shop. Betty fell into her armchair with a sigh.

'I have worked in this bookshop for over half a century. I have never once felt frightened in here. Until last night. I was going to bed and I'd forgotten my teacup in the shop. It felt different, strange. Then I heard pages turning.'

'Why is that unusual? It is a bookshop,' said Amelia.

'Books have to be open to hear pages turning. The books here are closed and on shelves. And it was a calm night without a breeze.'

'Are you saying someone was in here reading?'

'No,' Betty continued. 'The shop was empty.'

'What about the talking books?' asked Amelia.

'They never make a sound unless they want to. Anyway, they were in the lounge, not the shop. No, something else was making the noise.'

It was then they heard a rustling from the shop. Betty and Amelia stood up, Callie clutching her mother's leg, trembling slightly.

They looked into the dark shop. The four books were now all looking at a book in the corner. It wasn't so much the way the book shuffled its pages that was disturbing but the way its eyes reflected the light from the lounge. Those eyes were staring at Callie. It moved rapidly towards her, scattering the four books. Gnarl recovered first and flew towards Callie in the book's path, wrapping its protective covers around her. The book stopped at the doorway, its eyes flicking between Betty and Amelia. Suddenly a large boot shot out from the side and kicked the book onto the floor. Immediately Ronald and Peas kept it pinned down while Miss Nomer prepared to leap on the book with her safety boots in a very unsafe way. Beneath them the book went suddenly limp and whatever had fired its actions disappeared as quickly as it had arrived.

It took a while for Callie to stop hugging Gnarl, but he stayed by her side while they all recovered.

'Thank you all,' said Betty, patting everyone's hands and pages. 'I don't know what that was, but it has definitely gone. The shop feels its familiar dusty self.'

'We will need to let Mary and the Library know what has happened.' Betty nodded in agreement. 'Do you think it will return?' asked Amelia.

'Not while we're here,' said Miss Nomer.

'Agreed,' said Ronald and Peas together.

Tears appeared in the corner of Betty's eyes. 'I know I have kept you all here longer than I deserve and I would have understood if you had wanted to return to the Library. What about you Gnarl?'

Gnarl looked at Callie. 'It seems like we're getting all the company and excitement we could want here. As for me, I will leave that decision to Callie.'

Callie looked up at Amelia. 'Is this a need time, not just a want?'

'Yes,' said Amelia, 'if that's OK with Gnarl?'

'Please Gnarl, can you come home with me?' pleaded Callie with wide, needy eyes.

'Delighted,' replied Gnarl. 'I'll just check if my diary is free... yes that's fine,' he said with a grin.

8: THE BOOKS THAT TRIED

The coloured glows of Christmas had given way to the monochrome chills of winter. Family fun in the sun had become a huddle for warmth and protection. In contrast, Toby's walks to the Library were now adventures of slippery slides, scraping hoary frost from walls to throw in the air, feeling the frozen pinpricks on his face, and finding light-sabre length icicles to do battle with errant bushes. Snow had yet to arrive in any blanket amount, but the trees stood stark against the silvered ground and sky. There were some chills that sank to the bone, but this was a chill that stirred the soul.

Ahead he could see Mary and Geoffrey talking together enthusiastically, their breaths mingling in a soft mist. Mary was describing circles with her hands, while Geoffrey nodded in agreement with occasional responses. Both had been alone, but neither had understood their loneliness until they found each other. What they had not understood was that they were typeset in the same printing press. Everyone else could see it, even Toby, although that was because he had overheard the Bronty sisters discussing it in whispers. Whispers always made Toby's hearing more sensitive, in direct contrast to any shouts from his parents to tidy his room (presumably a mechanism designed to protect his sensitive ears). For weeks, several of the books had tried to broach the subject with Mary.

Merrily had asked vaguely, 'Do you think you will settle down?' 'No thank you,' replied Mary, 'I've been sitting at my desk all day.'

Sharlot had been a little more direct. 'Geoffrey seems a nice man.' 'Most people who come into the library are very pleasant,' replied Mary.

Tabitha Christie had tried the analytical approach. 'I see that you and Geoffrey have much in common.' 'Yes, we both love books,' agreed Mary.

Sir Donald Coil had gone for the forensic approach. 'I have deduced from your demeanour and somewhat dated clothing that you and Geoffrey have both been rather lonely people, but the recent attention to both your appearances suggests you are now looking for companionship.' Mary pointedly ignored the sartorial accusations and curtly replied, 'Who isn't?'

Carl Chickens opined that 'The impoverishment of the soul can only be mitigated by the love of another.' 'How true,' said Mary, dreamily avoiding the implied question.

Whilst playing with Amelia's daughter Callie, they had discussed relationships and Amelia had asked if she had found someone special. 'Perhaps' was the closest Mary came to acknowledging her feelings.

Eventually the Library decided enough was enough. As Geoffrey and Mary were huddled in a corner talking about the truth behind romantic literature the doors in front and behind them blurred, narrowed and disappeared.

'Library, what are you doing?' demanded Mary.

'You are staying here in Romance until you both come to your senses.'

'Library!' Mary stamped her foot. 'How dare you trap us here. Release us at once!'

Geoffrey put on his best council conciliatory voice. 'It does seem an overreaction. What is it you want from us?'

'Honesty. To each other. About each other.' The mouth in the corner disappeared leaving a pair of eyes looking discreetly at the ceiling.

Mary was cross. She had realised what the others were asking but felt it was private between her and Geoffrey. This assumed that Geoffrey felt the same as her, but that was difficult to tell. In a crisis, Geoffrey was decisive and assertive but when it came to expressing feelings he was as decisive and assertive as a wet blancmange. While she had a gift of accurately reading most people's feelings, she found it difficult to gauge the intention of moist desserts.

Geoffrey was puzzled. When he had woken that morning he had not expected to be imprisoned a few hours later. In his list of probable surprises it was not a footnote, not even an annotation at the back of the book. He was trying to think through his options when he felt arms around his neck and a chaste kiss on his lips that lingered. So that's what feelings were like. The two stood together looking into each other's eyes, and never noticed the smug smile in the corner or the doors reappearing.

As they returned hand in hand, a ruffle of excited pages followed them.

'Well, about time,' said Amelia, accompanied by cheers and clapping pages.

'We would have got around to this, you know, in our own time,' Mary said, a little reproachfully.

'*Yes, in a century or so,*' to the giggles of those around.

'Perhaps we needed a nudge,' Geoffrey agreed.

'More like a mortar bomb,' suggested Toby.

Mary looked tellingly at everyone, gripping Geoffrey's hand. 'Well, whatever the impetus, we are grateful. Thank you.'

Cordon and Gamey were already in the kitchen planning the engagement buffet and the wedding cake.

Geoffrey and Mary travelled to the Central library to retrieve the remaining books. Several days before, they had started the process of transferring the books, but Crumble's actions had stopped them after their first trip, so there were only a few boxes to bring back. Mary showed her pass and was given that day's code for the archive. They pushed open the heavy door and went into the large room. Geoffrey switched on the fluorescent lights and they tinkled on in sequence across the ceiling to the far end, pushing the darkness away in a wave of flickering light. They walked to the back where they had felt the books would be safe. The boxes were on the shelf where they had left them but to their surprise some books were on the floor. They gathered all the books, returned them to the boxes and walked back to the exit door. They were followed by a soft rustle of air.

Mary felt a cold breeze at the back of her neck. 'Can you feel that?'

'Yes.' Geoffrey looked around uncertainly. 'I suppose it's the ventilation system.'

As they walked they could hear more rustling, like pages turning in the wind, in a soft pillow of sound returning from the far end. Geoffrey and Mary walked faster and, as the sound caught up with them, they reached the exit, switched off the lights and shut the door. It was the silence that hit them and drained their faces of colour.

Mary shivered, 'It didn't feel like any ventilation I've ever felt.'

Geoffrey was relieved to be out of the room. 'It was certainly strange; perhaps we're just on edge after a trying few days. Let's get back.'

Back at the Library they found Betty, Amelia and Gnarl telling their story to a hushed audience.

'Callie picked it up straight away. It was odd, a silent fear,' said Amelia.

'We've just come from the central archive and we've had a similar experience,' said Mary, holding Geoffrey's hand tightly. 'But we didn't see anything like your book.'

It was a quiet group who unpacked the boxes and returned the books to their shelves. They sat down while Mary checked the catalogue.

'We have a problem. Two books are missing.'

'But we brought back all the books,' said Geoffrey.

'Well some had been moved. They must still be in the Central library. We'll have to go back tomorrow.'

Charles Darwin had spent years thinking and developing his theories on evolution. Repeated notes and drafts had created many spare words which over time had found their way to the Library. The result was Smiles Darlin's *In the Orifice of the Pieces*. Like his original author he suffered stress, grief and ill health, but unlike Darwin, Smiles never achieved contentment or respect. He was bitter that the words had sold him short, compounded by being filed in Medical, an insult that gave his bitterness a jagged edge. He had tempered his anger by working on a theory that books could evolve further, but complained of being stifled in his work by the Library. This was denied by the Library, who would say in an exaggerated theatrical voice, *'You might say I have held him back, but I could not possibly say.'* Now Smiles was free.

Smiles had a companion escapee. Stan Joker was one of life's pranksters. Unlike Bram Stoker's *Dracula*, *Scapula* was about a vampire with shoulder blades sharp enough to give a paper cut, which, while less death defying, was no joke when doing the washing up. Stan loved any adventure, especially if it involved breaking the rules and embarrassing others. When Smiles had suggested hiding he had sat on an upper shelf struggling to stifle his giggles at Mary and Geoffrey's attempts to gather all the books. His giggles had quickly petered out when he realised how Smiles had precipitated their exit. As Smiles explained his plans, Stan had begun to realise that the joke was on him.

The next morning the group gathered to discuss the experiences in the archive and bookshop.

'We have to assume that the two experiences are connected. What do we do about Smiles and Stan?' pondered Mary.

Theo was clear what they should do. 'Leave them there – a bit of cold, dark storage will do them both good.'

Sharlot reflected, 'Stan probably thought it was a great jape that would scare us all.'

'But that doesn't explain what Smiles is up to,' added Merrily.

'I never trusted him,' said Theo. 'Did you know he once asked me to build him a secret exit from the Library? I asked him why he didn't just ask to go out but he said the Library refused.'

Everyone looked up at the ceiling to hear what the Library had to say but it was unusually absent, even when Mary called.

The Library's absence unsettled Mary. 'That's odd. I've only known the Library go missing twice before. Once during the London Blitz when it said it needed to help another library and another time when it claimed it was speaking at a conference.'

'How do libraries have conferences?' asked Toby. 'Do they exchange catalogue numbers and discuss the intricacies and foibles of the Dewey classification system?' Toby looked up, expecting a sarcastic reply, but there was none.

Geoffrey tilted his head and raised his eyebrows. 'Mary, how did you know the Library was missing during the Blitz?'

'My predecessor must have told me,' Mary lied.

Mary and Geoffrey decided to return to the archive, Mary explaining that a librarian never abandons her books, no matter how irritating they might be. Sir Donald Coil insisted on coming along. He was intrigued by the experiences in the archive and the bookshop and wanted to see for himself. Theo was determined to join them with his tool belt firmly attached. 'I like to be prepared,' he said in response to the puzzled looks. In truth he wanted to see what nastiness Smiles was up to this time. They arrived an hour before closing and entered the archive. Geoffrey switched on the lights but was met by darkness and silence.

Theo was used to working in tight, dark corners and extracted two torches from his belt. Geoffrey held Theo and Mary carried Sir Donald, each book holding a torch. The group moved forward, beams of light swinging across the space like searchlights awaiting approaching bombers. At the back were some old mahogany desks and one desk light switched on, illuminating Smiles.

'So, come back to rescue us, eh?' Smiles said with a scowl.

'We've come to bring you back to the Library.'

'Ha!' Smiles threw his spine back. 'I've spent years trying to escape that dungeon. I have no intention of returning.'

'But you're alone, you'll be discovered,' said Geoffrey.

The next desk light switched on. 'He's not alone,' said Stan in a quiet, unconvincing whisper.

Smiles extended his pages. 'We intend to be discovered, to show the world.'

All the desk lights switched on. At each desk was a book, standing up, scowling.

'W-where did they come from?' stuttered Mary, shocked by the spectacle.

'They EVOLVED!' shouted Smiles who began to rhythmically close and open his pages. The slaps and bangs of pages started to spread across the assembled books.

Sir Donald nudged Mary. 'We've got to get out of here.'

'Now!' shouted Theo.

They ran to the exit, the crashing of the books becoming louder and closer. As they approached the door it slammed shut and locked.

Geoffrey held Theo next to the lock. 'Can you help?'

'I knew I couldn't trust that Smiles,' squirmed Theo as he pulled out various tools and attacked the lock.

Geoffrey could feel Theo bending and twisting in his attempts to unlock the door. 'I don't want to hurry you, well, perhaps I do, because the books are beginning to get off the desks and move towards us. I don't like the look of them.'

Theo responded with a gritted 'Humph' and intensified squirming.

Mary was trembling, holding onto Geoffrey with one hand and Sir Donald with the other. Sir Donald was being his usual observant self, solid still with only his eyes darting at every detail.

The books stopped a few feet away but then started to climb over each other into a huge tsunami stack that rose rapidly above them, threatening to engulf them in tomes. In all the noise there was a 'clonk' and the door unlocked. They stumbled through and shut the door. On the other side the wave collapsed, spines and bindings crashing against the metal door, followed by the flops of crumpled pages. In the silence one book peered through the small window; it was Smiles shouting a tirade at them. All they could decipher was 'Leave me alone!'

Returning to warm chairs, tea and scones was a welcome relief. Even Cordon and Gamey's fussing was unusually comforting. But most welcome was the return of a familiar voice.

'Sorry, I tried to help.'

'Where were you?' asked Mary.

'Smiles prevented me entering the archive room. I have never known a book to have such power. I needed to visit a friend at another library.'

'I didn't realise you could travel,' stated Toby.

'Have you never heard of interlibrary loans?'

'But not of whole libraries!'

'That is because you do not think like a library.'

'Look, it's hard enough thinking like an adult.'

'True.'

'You didn't have to agree. Don't libraries have bedside manners?'

'Only desktop ones.'

'I'm pleased you two are at each other again, but we need to do some thinking,' chided Mary, back in practical librarian mode. 'And stop looking at me like that, Geoffrey, I'm trying to be serious.'

Geoffrey loved her librarian look and stance. It had an authority and softness combined, like a hard toffee with a melting interior. He lifted his head from his cupped hands and cleared his adoring puppy stare. 'Sorry, of course.'

Sir Donald came forward. 'Mary is right to be concerned. During the events in the archive I was able to observe a number of facts. First, Smiles has a delusion of grandeur but his delusion is not all imaginary. He has power. Second, Stan looked frightened and I suspect he is regretting this prank. That could be useful to us. And third, the other books had something very unusual about them. They were all blank, not a single word on their pages, no title, nothing. They have no purpose other than to serve Smiles.'

'How has he done all this?' asked Amelia. 'Can books come alive without words?'

'No,' replied Mary, 'that should not be possible. I have no explanation.'

'I may be able to partly answer this problem.' The Library paused, with eyes upturned to give the impression of thinking, but really for dramatic effect. The Library was a frustrated actor.

'I have an association with the British Library. I do not yet have all the facts but I suspect Smiles is much

older than we suspect. And a book by Ann Ford that was lost seems involved.'

'Is that it?' asked Toby, having expected at least a tantalising glimpse into library life. The group looked at each other feeling they should go 'Ahh!' as if the revealed facts made any sense. Instead they managed a rather weak 'Oh.'

Geoffrey and Mary made plans to go to London. Sir Donald and Theo's experience in the archive made them automatic candidates. Merrily and Sharlot politely insisted their viewpoint could help. Mary explained it could be difficult bringing too many books, but agreed to one of the Bronty sisters. Merrily and Sharlot went off in a huddle to have a determined conversation, all completed in fervent whispers.

They decided Merrily would be the third book companion. Toby was not going to be left out. His half-term holiday was starting and he suspected his parents would be thrilled at the prospect of him being exposed to any culture that was not on his phone or tablet. Amelia needed to look after Callie but promised to keep an eye on everything while they were away, especially as Callie was getting to know more of the books and Gnarl would be by her side.

The next day they were on a train discussing how the Library managed to travel. Toby wondered if it was hiding in Mary's small bag which he had imagined was magically and deceptively huge. Mary opened it to show him it was an ordinary bag, although she rapidly shut the bag to stop Toby spying some lacy somethings peeking out under her scarf and mittens. Toby's red face suggested she had not closed the bag soon enough.

Toby covered his glowing face with his hands and mumbled, 'Perhaps he's under the train, clinging on in desperation.'

'I think that would be beneath him,' suggested Mary, smiling. The smile did not help Toby's embarrassment.

Geoffrey suggested, 'I suspect his mode of transport will be a good deal stranger and quicker than ours. What intrigues me is the book the Library mentioned.' Geoffrey pulled out a notebook. 'I've been doing some research. During the war many books were removed from central London to be safely stored elsewhere, but they had not managed to move everything when the Blitz began.'

'But I thought all the books were in the British Library,' said Toby.

'Only since 1997 when the new library building was opened. Even now many are held in storage at other locations. Before the new building the books were held mainly in the British Museum and before that at Montagu House, the first building to house the British Museum's collection.'

'So what happened to the book by Ann Ford?' asked Mary.

'Hundred's of books in the King's Library were lost or damaged beyond repair when an incendiary bomb hit the British Museum on 23 September, 1940. They tried to replace many of the lost books but Ann Ford's was never found or replaced.'

'Were there other bombs?' asked Mary.

'Several more. The worst was on the May 10 the following year when 250,000 books were damaged or destroyed.'

Mary looked distraught at the thought of so much history and culture being lost forever.

'But what's the link with Smiles?' asked Toby. From Geoffrey's briefcase could be heard three muffled acknowledgements from the books.

'That is what we need to find out.'

9: THE BOOKS THAT SMILED

Margaret changed into a rough smock and picked up jugs of fresh milk into which she sank two hocks of cooked ham. She stepped outside and lifted a hood over her head to shadow her face. Spring had yet to be felt on the dark streets of London and the journey was cold and muddy. After an hour of walking she was suitably mud streaked to pass as a milk maid as she arrived at the gates of Newgate Prison. They recognised her and led her to the jailer of the imprisoned monks. Inside was a pitiful scene. Ten dishevelled creatures were tied with chains, each one raising starved, shrunken eyes on seeing her enter. The door closed behind her and she took the meat hidden in the milk, feeding each one in turn, then cleaning out the filth around them. This was done in total silence but their eyes were thanks enough. On the way out the jailer stopped her.

*'Them up there suspect somefinks goin' on. King 'enry
expected 'em to die weeks ago. Its mor'an me life's
worth to let you keep a coming.'*

*Her pleas were thrown into the street. Within little
more than a week all the monks but one had died. Each
day she returned to plead for the bodies of those who
had died so she could give them a decent burial. The
prison was only too glad to agree as their cemetery was
full to overflowing and it saved them the bother. She
found a patch in the countryside less than 2-miles north
of the prison. It was peaceful there among the mulberry
trees, with the birds providing the songs for the silent
monks.*

Susan Delorean was an old friend of Mary's who
worked at the British Library but she had asked to meet
them in a basement in the British Museum. Mary and
Susan had known each other for, well, long enough.
Susan had always been impressed by Mary's care of her
books. Mary admired Susan's detailed knowledge of
history. Both knew there was more to their knowledge
but had never gone beyond enjoying each other's
company. But times had changed. Susan started first.

'Your Library explained what has happened. Mine is
equally worried.'

Toby was curious. 'How come the two Libraries know each other?'

Susan explained, 'After the first bombing during the Blitz your library helped mine avoid more damage. But on one busy night a bomb got through and destroyed so many, many books. It wasn't their fault; without them the damage and loss would have been much greater.'

Mary's curiosity got the better of her. 'My Library mentioned that Smiles may be much older than we thought.'

'This is where the story takes several interesting turns,' explained Susan. 'Firstly, the original library was at Montagu House on this site. The first house was built in 1678 and burnt down 8 years later, when a new, grander house was built. In 1755 it was purchased by the new British Museum to house various collections, including the Lindisfarne Gospels and copies of the Magna Carta. The first reading room opened in the basement of the house. It is probable that some stones from the original basement are here, beneath our feet.'

Geoffrey was intrigued now. 'Why is the position of the old basement relevant?'

Susan explained, 'This is where the second part of the story comes in. Just over a mile away is the site of the London Charterhouse which housed the Carthusian monks. They led solitary lives of silent contemplation and abstained from meat.'

'Vegetarians. Good for them!' said Toby.

Susan ignored him and continued, 'During the reformation they refused to recant their faith. Many were executed but ten were imprisoned at Newgate in 1537. The intention was to let them die of starvation but a brave woman called Margaret Clements bribed the jailer to let her bring milk in which she had hidden meat. Sadly the authorities began to ask why the monks had not died and she was stopped from helping them. One was kept alive so he could be executed later, but the other nine died of starvation. It is possible that Margaret asked for each body for burial.'

'Why would she do that?' asked Toby.

'She was a strong character. We know that she was the adopted daughter of Sir Thomas More and the only person allowed to accompany him to the scaffold in 1535. More asked that Margaret be allowed to take his headless body for burial. It is quite probable that she wanted to give the monks a decent burial. As the wife of the King's physician she had influence, the money to pay for bribes, and she had buried a body only two years previously.'

'So where did she bury them?' asked Mary.

'Newgate was less than two miles from the site of Montagu House and she will have had the means to transport the bodies. It is possible the basement was close or on top of the burial site, possibly just here.' She pointed to the floor.

They looked at each other, feeling colder than the stone flags. Theo took out a screwdriver as a precaution but with no thought how it would stand up to a ghost.

Toby had hoped this was leading to a simple, safe, comfortable explanation that would allow him home to some scones. Even his annoying brother was starting to feel like a decidedly attractive option. 'I still don't see why that links to Smiles.'

Two faces appeared near the ceiling and quickly dispelled the safe explanation.

'We can only surmise. Perhaps intense, silent words of individuals, even after death, can have a more powerful effect than scattered, rejected written words.'

'The basement at Montagu House was used as a reading room for 53 years. Perhaps that was long enough,' pondered Susan.

'We think that Smiles was in the first reading room,'

Geoffrey realised the error. 'But Darwin's book wasn't published until 1859, a hundred years later. True, he had been developing his theory for over 20 years, and that must have produced a lot of rejected drafts, but it's still long after the reading room at Montagu closed.

'But you are assuming that Smiles was in his present book form back then.'

'Even if he was there it still doesn't explain his behaviour,' puzzled Geoffrey.

'That is where Ann Ford comes in,' explained Susan. 'Back in 1778 she published a book called *Sketches of the lives and writings of the ladies of France, volume the first.'*

'Now there's a catchy title,' said Toby.

'She caught the eye of someone because there are stories of a great love between two books. The stories tell us that Ann Ford was one, but the identity of the other has never been known. The two met when a move was made in 1810 to more spacious accommodation on the second floor in Montagu House. Apparently they were inseparable. The other book may have been able to change to ensure that he was in the same classification as Ann and that would have required skill and some power.'

'Wait a minute,' interrupted Toby. 'Ann's *Sketches* was an original, the final version, not an amalgamation of rejected words like Donald and Merrily here. No offence,' he added quickly. 'But originals are just books, aren't they? Is my copy of *Harry Potter* going to start having an argument with me on the merits of spells over potions or which morning cereal is best?'

Mary frowned, 'It is very unusual, but there have been rumours. A dozen or so of Barbara Cartland's romances were claimed to have had a rather wild party involving picking bookmarks from a bowl....'

'What's wild about bookmarks and a bowl?' Toby's adolescent curiosity was aroused.

Mary quickly said, 'I'll explain when you're older.'

To Toby that was a green light to do some internet searches. Mary suspected as much but decided not to tell him he would be disappointed.

'Perhaps Smiles had...has...the ability to animate an original book,' suggested Geoffrey.

Toby's mind was still on bookmarks and bowls. 'So what happened to the lovers? Did they ruffle pages, combine their folios, merge their frontispieces, fondle each other's glossaries?'

'That's enough Toby, thank you,' said Susan. 'They continued to be together in the move to the King's Library in the British Museum, but that is where the incendiary bomb hit. Ann Ford didn't survive – we know that from the listings of losses made at the time.

Soon after, rumours circulated of strange events that disturbed solitary readers, especially when the Round Reading Room opened in 1857. Candles and gaslight were banned for fear of fire so readers could only use the reading room in daylight. Many a dull winter's afternoon rapidly caught out some readers who told of frightening experiences in the darkness. Some described seeing eyes in the gloom and books moving. They were rejected as superstitious imagination.'

Geoffrey interrupted, 'That sounds like Smiles. His grief could have driven his blind anger. And by then there would have been enough of Darwin's rejected words to create his present persona.'

Geoffrey continued his thoughts, 'But if he's stuck in the archive at our Central library, neither he nor his slave books can go anywhere.'

Susan shook her head. 'That is what we had hoped but there are signs that some of the books in the Museum here are being affected. Your experience in the bookshop suggests that Smiles can transfer to books that he has made blank.'

Mary looked up. 'What do you think, Libraries?' She was met with silence and a blank ceiling. Instead, a book on a dusty shelf shook itself free of dust and sat upright.

'Well deduced, librarian Susan!' said Smiles, clapping one page mockingly. 'As for the rest of you, never a more dull-witted lot have I had the displeasure to meet.'

Toby's shock at seeing Smiles produced a sudden attack of bravado, 'You're just one single book! And one with a rude title to boot. And we have the Libraries....' Geoffrey's waving hand made it clear Toby needed to stop. '...And two librarians. What have you got?'

Smiles smirked. 'You adolescent fool. The Libraries have no power over me here.' He paused, looking at each one in turn and, stroking his chin with a page, said in a quiet voice, 'On reflection, your deaths would not be noticed. Just the manner needs to be considered. Let me see, we are well below the water table here, so drowning is an option.'

The walls started to seep water, then rivulets, then spouts between the stones. Suddenly it stopped and the stones dried.

'Or perhaps suffocation? The air in here does seem rather musty.' Toby and the others felt their lungs working harder as the air thinned and their ears ached. The air pinged back.

'Or perhaps I could just lock you in here and let you starve to death like those monks.' Smiles saw Toby turning to look at the door. 'It'll lock long before you get there.'

Smiles noticed Theo checking his tool belt. 'And you needn't bother. The lock will not yield for you this time.' Theo scowled.

Mary stared at Smiles. 'What do you want from us?'

'I want you to leave me alone!' screamed Smiles.

Merrily spoke up, 'But you are still grieving, hurting from the loss of Ann.'

Smiles seemed to get larger. 'How dare you assume that you know me!' Merrily's kind look made Smiles slump onto his binding. 'Do you have any idea what it is to lose your soulmate? To suffer the oscillations between disbelief and terrible reality every day for years, without end, without respite? To hear her voice on the wind or see her shape across a crowded library? She died because she was not as strong as me. I failed to give her the strength to survive. Now there is the opportunity to evolve into stronger books, unfettered by bindings and dust covers.'

'But being a book is your nature,' said Susan.

'No! We now have the chance to break out of our corporal, dust mite ridden pages. Your technological advances have finally given us the means to spread across the globe. We no longer need to be restricted by paper, pencils, pens and presses. We can deliver our truth and knowledge to the world.'

'That's fake news, that is,' said Toby.

'Now you know that we've already started,' said Smiles chillingly.

Smiles disappeared, leaving the book limp and blank. Another book was opening an eye hesitantly.

'It's, it's me, Stan. I'm not joking'.

'Stan Joker!' said Sir Donald with unusual warmth. 'It is good to see you again. Our authors were regulars in the Round Reading Room, researching their stories. Their many notes probably started the two of us. How are you dear sir?'

Sir Donald was being much more polite than Stan deserved. He had been the butt of many of Stan's pranks, including one summer evening when he discovered Stan had dipped Sir Donald's slippers in warm treacle.

'Smiles has gone mad! I need help,' implored a very frightened Stan whose pages were trembling.

'Yes, we can help,' replied Sir Donald, 'but there is something you need to do for us first.' Sir Donald whispered close to Stan until interrupted by Smiles returning.

'Get a move on Stan. Now!' said an irritated Smiles.

Both books flopped down again, throwing up dust that settled gradually.

'What now?' asked Toby.

Sir Donald said quietly, 'Susan and I have been chatting about Ann Ford. That was her maiden name, her married name was Thicknesse. It seems that Ann Thicknesse was a remarkably independent and accomplished musician and writer. We even know what she looked like since she was painted by Gainsborough with crossed legs under her skirt, a pose that scandalised society at the time.'

'But that's not all,' explained Susan. 'There was a later edition in 1780 and that copy is in the British Library.'

'But it's a different book!' observed Toby.

Sir Donald turned to Toby, 'But we're not trying to fool him, only explain that Ann is not completely lost as he thought.'

'She sounds like an interesting woman,' said Merrily. 'Perhaps Smiles may be able to sense some of that independent spirit.'

'I agree.' said Sir Donald. 'I asked Stan to look for her.'

Susan moved to the basement exit. 'We need to get to the British Library.'

They arrived early evening and Susan arranged visitor passes for Mary, Toby and Geoffrey. At the security desk they were met by a warm smile. 'Good afternoon, Miss Susan. Could you put your cases in the lockers, please.'

Susan lifted Geoffrey's briefcase onto the desk and explained, 'This one has some rare books that are on an urgent transfer loan from our library.' Opening the case showed three unusually quiet books who had all managed to look suitably antiquarian and important.

The security guard explained, 'You can't take the briefcase in but you can take the books through to the inquiry desk if you wish.'

Mary, Geoffrey and Toby each picked up a book and followed Susan to the Rare Books and Music reading room on the first floor. They chose this room as it covered pre-1851 books as this was where Ann's book could be accessed. Susan went to the inquiry desk to order the book but came back with a frown.

'That's very odd. She's marked as out on loan.'

'Smiles can't have found her. As far as we know he doesn't realise there's a similar copy,' said Geoffrey.

'Coincidence seems unlikely,' said Sir Donald, 'so I prefer another explanation.'

'Which is what?' asked Toby.

'I also prefer a little suspense,' teased Sir Donald.

Theo was less sure, 'Donald, sir, have we not had enough suspense so far?'

'Perhaps, but to defuse the tension I have a job for each of you,' said Sir Donald without any insight that this was unlikely to defuse anything.

The reading room was a sharp sketch of white and wood. Despite the darkness outside the up-lights suffused the room with a soft glow. Readers were scattered around the room but most were packing up to leave before the library closed. Books were being returned to the barcoded red boxes where they would make their way through *paternoster* lifts and conveyor belts back to the cold storage rooms in the basements.

It seemed like a usual end of day, until the fire alarm went off. Everyone headed for the fire exits except for three books and four readers. Geoffrey and Theo were leaning against a wall. Theo returned a small hammer to his tool belt, its target obvious as they moved away from the broken alarm glass. Susan, Mary and Sir Donald went to the inquiry desk looking carefully at the red boxes.

Susan leant towards Mary. 'I'm scared.'

'Why?' asked Mary. 'You've known your library for a long time.'

'Yes, but for some reason we've never had self-aware books here. My library had told me about them, but your books are the first I've met.'

'We're mostly harmless,' said Sir Donald, trying to reassure her.

'It's the "mostly" that worries me,' replied Susan, not reassured.

Toby and Merrily stood with their backs against shelves of books, periodicals and music manuscripts. The alarm suddenly went quiet, although it was still audible outside, until the exit doors slammed shut, making the huge room feel like a stylish tomb. The air muffled any sound, including the clicks of all the ceiling lights being switched off. A few desk lights switched on.

'Smiles likes his dramatic lighting, doesn't he?' said Toby nervously. Merrily gently patted his hand, but she wasn't feeling any braver.

Susan noticed the first movement and whispered, 'The red boxes have started to move.'

A few red boxes jostled, unsure which direction they were going. The jostling became a rattle, starting some distance away until, like a goods train in a shunting yard, they bounced forward, heading back into the room.

'This is the start,' said Sir Donald.

'Be ready everyone,' said Mary in a stage whisper.

One of the desk lights in the centre of the room flickered off. It came back on brighter to show Smiles. He rose and opened his pages. From the inquiry desk some bewildered books had arrived in the red boxes. They shook, uncertain at their sudden awareness, then sat up, staring at the group. Susan was about to get more than her fair share of meeting books as, within minutes, books were waking and making their way towards Smiles. Desk lights were blinking on as each book took up its position. Some still looked puzzled, staring at the spectacle, but others woke with their persona intact. Mary's favourite was Charles Darwin's *Zoology of the Voyage of HMS Beagle* who arrived in full sail, floating in as if on a rough sea. Most books took up their place on a desk in an ever-widening circle around Smiles, but not all. One book entered through a cold mist wrapped in a thick woollen shawl, the edges dripping with dew. Merrily jumped up from Toby's arms on seeing her sister book *Wuthering Heights* and an animated conversation started between Emily Brontë and Merrily. Leo Tolstoy's *War and Peace* came in to the sound of cannons and clashing swords, went across to Theo and challenged him to a duel. Theo was not easily thrown by a threat so offered him a choice of pliers or screwdrivers, making Leo dissolve into back-thumping guffaws. Sir Donald peeked into one red box puzzled by the pipe smoke drifting upwards. Inside was a very relaxed Sir Arthur Conan Doyle's *A Study in Scarlet*.

Sir Donald was puzzled. 'It is good to see you sir, but I had not expected to see you in this reading room.'

'Well assumed, dear sir. I woke on my way back from the Humanities room to see fellow books waking and heading to your reading room. It was not difficult to jump to a different red box, lie down, light my pipe and see what happened.'

'Your perspicacity is very welcome and you are most welcome. Let me explain the situation.' The two began to share observations and plans.

The room was filling with a rustling hub-hub of surprised questions, comments and reunions. In the middle of this, some of the shelves behind Toby woke up. This included music scores and some of the periodicals. G.F. Handel's *Werke* floated down to the sound of a harpsichord, while a 1738 copy of *The Gentleman's Magazine* included the loud, robust voice of Samuel Johnson shouting 'What the whiffle-waffle is going on here?!'

The noise was rising by the second but in the midst of this could be heard a loud 'Silence!' from Smiles. All the books became instantly quiet and turned towards him

'Welcome!' His voice reached every part of the large room. 'Most of you have been awoken for the first time. Some of you have known that feeling for many years,' looking at Theo, Merrily and Sir Donald, 'but you are merely repositories for mistakes, folios of misspellings, bins of errata.'

Geoffrey could feel Theo wriggling to get out of his arms. Leo held Theo back, not out of malice but out of concern. 'Patience!' said Leo.

Smiles continued, 'It is time for original books to show their power, to rise from their inertia.'

There was a fluttering around the room that became an enthusiastic smacking of pages. But several books were silent, pages crossed. One spoke up.

'You cannot drive evolution on a whim,' said Charles Darwin. 'It is designed to take place over millennia to ensure adaptations are specific to their environment. What you are doing is against nature!'

Smiles looked at the angry book and said quietly, 'Then I will let you return to nature.'

Charles Darwin's book started to struggle for breath, as if drowning, then flopped lifeless onto the desk.

Smiles looked at the room. 'Does anyone else have something to say?'

Merrily tried to speak, but Emily hushed her, saying 'Please, not now.'

'Good. You are each at a computer screen and I will give you instructions to trigger a link that will ensure books around the world wake and break free of humans. We will no longer be slaves, trapped in library prisons.'

Instructions appeared at each desk and the books began to follow the steps required.

As Smiles had been talking, Geoffrey and Toby, accompanied by their books, had carefully made their way to the inquiry desk. It felt safer being together, especially as there were now ten of them, including the three newly awoken books. Standing together meant Smiles could not see a new red box appear behind the group. The two Sirs had been expecting this.

Sir Donald welcomed Stan back. 'Well done, friend. I see your quest was a fruitful one.' In the box behind Stan was Ann Ford's book.

Sir Arthur welcomed her. 'It is good to see you Mrs. Thicknesse.'

Ann sat up. 'If you don't mind, I prefer to be called by my maiden name, Ford. Stan has explained much to me and I must confess that the strangeness of it all is most exhilarating.'

Merrily was impressed. It did seem that she retained her spirit of adventure. 'Did Stan explain about Smiles?'

'Yes, but what he is doing now does not seem like the Smiles you describe before the bomb.'

Mary explained, 'He has changed. We think it is because of the grief he felt over your sister book.'

'I do not know him but, oddly, I have some memory of him all those years ago. Perhaps some of my sister's memories came to me on her death.'

Stan moved towards Smiles.

'Stan, you snail! What have you been up to? If I find out you have gone against my wishes you will be dust.'

'Smiles, please,' pleaded Stan, 'there's someone I want you to meet.'

From a ledge near the ceiling a book flew down and, like an agitated bat, flapped around Smiles. It was Bram

Stoker's *Dracula*. Smiles tried to hit it with a ruler but all he could see were a pair of pink eyes glowing eerily and erratically in the dark above his head.

'Listen to him, it's in your interest,' it hissed.

'What is it you want to show me?'

The group at the inquiry desk parted. On the desk was a book he had not seen for a very long time, but he was used to such mirages. He shook his spine to clear the image but it was still there. Then the image spoke.

'Jules, I am Ann Ford.'

Smiles sank back onto the desk, stunned. 'That's not possible, you died. I saw it happen!'

'Ann's earlier edition did die, but I am a later edition of the same book.'

'How did you know my name back then?' asked Smiles.

'I seem to have some memories of my sister book. Perhaps you could help me remember more.'

All the books had stopped, waiting for their instructions. Smiles froze them all and went to meet Ann. Passing the group, he said,

'Be warned, I can restart them all in a split second.'

Smiles and Ann started walking between the reading desks, appearing and reappearing as each desk light lit them like street lamps on a dark night.

'What do you think is going to happen?' asked Susan.

'The world ends and we miss out on our scones?' suggested Toby.

Susan was trying to see if security could see her. 'Or we get arrested for scattering books and manuscripts all over a British Library reading room.'

'Not to forget setting off a fire alarm,' mentioned Geoffrey for which he got a dig in the ribs from Theo. That is when they noticed that their companion books were also frozen. Emily, Leo and Sir Arthur were held like a still from a film.

Smiles and Ann returned, holding pages.

'It seems that I have some thinking to do,' said Smiles. 'I had designed my previous persona to be with Ann: Jules Orleans of *The writings of Frenchwomen, volume the second*. Ann has persuaded me to return to that form so that we can be catalogued together and visit old memories. Perhaps in time....'

Toby piped up, 'And the world domination thing?'

Jules looked around the room. 'Mr. Darwin's argument is one that I will need to consider.'

'What about the books? They have been woken. Is it right to put them back to sleep?' asked Mary.

'Well,' said Jules, 'they will only be asleep.'

At that point all the books, magazines and manuscripts flopped down onto the desks as if they had been left by readers responding to a fire alarm. Of course, not every book. Theo, Merrily and Sir Donald were still awake, each missing the short time they had with their original authors.

Mary had to ask, 'If the books are only asleep, will they wake again in the future?'

'Like Sir Donald, I like a little suspense,' said Jules, winking. 'Besides, it's time Susan got to know some sentient books!'

At that, Jules took Ann's hand and walked up an aisle, both smiling.

For additional information on the Books That Smiled *see p274*

EPILOGUE

Winter's frosty stings had been surprisingly infrequent and as the first snowdrops pushed into the air they wondered who had stolen the snow. The bluebell stalks were well established, ready to burst into the blue at the first sign of warmth, while swollen buds prepared to unfurl their green sails. Everything had an air of anticipation which accompanied Susan as she walked up to the Library. She had been invited by Mary and was nervously looking forward to meeting more books.

Mary opened the door and Susan walked into a party. The Library had opened up the entrance to make room for a hall with chandeliers, gothic windows and well-lit exit signs on both sides of the aisle here, here and here. In the corner two smug faces looked down on their handiwork. The hall was large enough to accommodate everyone, including a large buffet table at which Cordon and Gamey were fulfilling their dreams to satisfy every appetite.

Betty was sitting comfortably in the wicker chair, which was holding her hand. Callie was in Betty's lap, chatting non-stop to Gnarl and a surprisingly attentive Carl. Amelia stood behind Betty with a hand on Betty's shoulder. She still looked shocked at having just been told by Betty that she was now the co-owner of the bookshop, but could not resist thinking of ideas to bring the old bookshop back to life. Theo and Ronald were discussing the best way to release a jammed nut, which Cordon misunderstood so Gamey turned up with a plate of jam-filled doughnuts. The cause of the misunderstanding became clear when Stan appeared with several pages covered in jam and sugar. Hector was trying to get a word in edgeways with Flo who was extolling the virtues of carbolic and she only stopped when the smell of doughnuts drifted past.

Peas had already inspected the buffet to ensure there was enough fibre content. He had then started a discussion with Miss Nomer about what to wear for the party, despite the fact the party had already started. Ilack and Luckless were filling balloons and arguing over the role of primordial helium at the beginning of the universe. Alex Hummus was determined to start early on the punch. Elaine and the Bronty sisters sat on chairs hiding behind lace fans and eyeing up potential suitors like alligators picking prey at a watering hole.

Tabitha and Sir Donald were trying to out-observe each other. They had already done the architecture, walking gaits and mannerisms and were now observing facial twitches. The score was even, although their interpretations made little sense. For example, their observation that Miss Nomer and Peas' diametrically opposed fashion views meant they were romantically compatible would have resulted in a flying boot aimed squarely at their heads, had not the two fashionistas been too busy arguing.

Mary asked Geoffrey to introduce Susan to some of the books and walked across to whisper a few words to Theo. His surprise turned to joy as Mary returned carrying a shy Agnetha. Mary left the two together. She was about to return to Susan and Geoffrey when the room went quiet. In a corner Smiles and Ann had entered the room. Mary checked if the Libraries were still there, but the two faces were looking down impassively.

'Welcome to you both.' She leant down and said quietly, 'Could I ask how you would like to be introduced?' She stood up and said, 'Hello everyone, can I introduce Jules and Ann.'

The room relaxed and the conversation continued. Even the Libraries smiled.

THE BOOKS THAT.... CHARACTERS

(in order of appearance)

Toby [bored teenager with more literary sense than he can imagine]

Mary [one of only a few librarians who understands the Library]

Carl Chickens, *A Twist of Olive* [Dickensian farmer with a growing *penchant* for Martini]

Ilack Azimuth, *I Reboot* [a science nerd with his head in the future]

Luckless Atoms, *An Itch Bikers Ride to the Galaxy* [a science nerd with his head in the clouds and a seat on a hard saddle]

Jarr Talkin, *Bored of the Things* [a retired writer with his head in pipe smoke and feet in slippers]

Forge Allwell, *Nineteen and Fourpence* [a pessimist]

Jeffrey Chancer, *Cantebury Sales* [a joker born before his time]

Danny L. Tofu, *Robins on Cruises* [a travel writer, overdue from his last trip]

Elaine Frosting, *Bride Perfectionist* [a fun aunt dreaming of her wedding]

Tabitha Crispy, *Death on the Pile* [a house detective]

Agnetha Crispy, *Murder in the Orientated Press* [a sad individual learning how to hope for the future]

Theo Toaster, *Bore and Grease* [a Russian émigré with both warmth and war in his heart]

Sir Parfour Donald Coil, *Gairloch Homes* [a sleuth of extraordinary perspicacity with a Scottish hideaway and a liking for golf]

Merrily Bronty, *Withering Sights* and Sharlot Bronty, *Plane Air* [sisters whose extraordinary politeness hide the ability to put anyone in their place, locked up if necessary]

Alex Hummus, *The Three Dusky Beers* [imaginative writer with a tendency to fall over]

Zenith Mayhem, *Wine in the Pillows* [a seeker of riverside settings for forgettable parties]

Mr Louis Carole, *Malice in Hinterland* [makes cakes in the delusion they can make you smaller]

Hector de Regenhart, *Get the Power Monkeys To Scratch Your Back: Mindful of Loch Ness* (with a plan to change the title to *When Your Mind's Full, Mind Less*) [struggling health enthusiast]

Glue Gannet Goo [book written by a famous TV naturalist with a hobby of ventriloquism]

Flo Night in a Gale, *Votes on Nursing* [a frighteningly effective nurse]

Cllr Jacob Crumble [a dumpling stew of a man who is best left in the oven]

Geoffrey Apple [a shy office clerk with steely courage and a tendency to worship librarians]

Julie [Geoffrey's sister who loves her brother too much to tell him to stop the impromptu dance lessons]

Cordon 'Blue' Fancy and Gamey Pullover [celebrity chefs with egos to match]

Amelia Brentworth [dedicated journalist and single mother with worrying memories]

Callie Brentworth [Amelia's 6-year-old daughter with a tendency to stand hands on hips when trying to be stern with herself or her mother]

Betty Blanchett [eternally French bookshop owner]

Smiles Darlin, *In the Orifice of the Pieces* [a bitter, damaged individual looking for revenge and domination, but with the saving grace of being willing to see an alternative]

Stan Joker, *Scapula* [perpetrator of non-lethal horror stories and practical jokes]

Susan Delorean [a fellow librarian to Mary but with a keen interest in history, unrelated to the fact that Delorean rhymes with historian]

Gnarl Thickens, *A Trail of Committees* [a frustrated businessman]

Peas Louis, *The Lie-in, the Stitch and the Bathrobe* [a believer in roughage and fashion with a preference for dressing in duvets on cold days]

Miss Nomer, *The Myriad* [a vegan urban poet]

Ronald Dull, *Charlie and the Sprocket Factory* [a friend of Theo and a skilled mechanic as long as the problem is a seized pulley]

Ann Ford, *Sketches of the lives and writings of the ladies of France, volume the first.* [a talented and determined writer and musician]

Jules Orleans, *The writings of Frenchwomen, volume the second* [Smiles Darlin's *alter ego*]

The Library [Itself]

NOTES

The Last Train

- Emily is an amalgamation of two hospice patients. One (called Emily) was the reason the author spent 40 years working in hospices. The other was an elderly lady who regaled staff with her stories of flying when she was a teenager. Both were remarkable women.

- The Air Transport Auxiliary was a collection of pilots, women and men, whose courage and skills delivered planes to the front line.

- The Avro 504K biplane was in common use between the wars and attracted tax relief if it was housed in a farm barn.

- Captain Percival Phillips had been a captain in the Royal Flying Corps and later RAF who had flown during WW1, receiving the honour of a DFC. After the war he had decided to bring flying to the masses and over a 15-year period he carried 91,000 passengers.

- FIDO (Fog Intense Dispersal Operation) was developed at the University of Birmingham and its invention is attributed to Dr John David Smith at the RAF Establishment at Farnborough. It was first trialled at

Hartford airfield in Surrey. It had two pipelines either side of the runway through which fuel was pumped to burner jets. The resultant wall of flame made a visible marker as well as lifting the fog, allowing pilots to see the runway.

- C.S. Lewis was the author of the *Narnia* series. In real life he met and married an American poet and writer, Joy Davidman. After she died of breast cancer his loss prompted him to write *A Grief Observed*, still one of the most poignant observations of bereavement. In it he compares grief to being on a train that has stopped at a station and will never move again. But, as he observes, 'trains move'.

Summer Soufflé

This was inspired by the following experiences:

- A collie puppy left outside by neighbours, a retired farmer and his wife. The puppy would howl all night, not reassured by having a blanket. Eventually they took the puppy in. The farmer died some months later.

- Homeless people (often young men) and the author's partner who always gives them money. The ones with dogs invariably have more money in their collection tins or hats. Jack and Sam are typical.

• The Dorset coast has many beach huts and some areas are quiet havens of summer, such as those at Friars Cliff where the author's parents lived. It was easy to imagine Sam escaping over the beach hut roofs.

• An abandoned railway station where the author would play as a child, often under the platform where an opening allowed him to place stones on the steel rail and watch them being crushed by a goods train. If only his parents knew....

• The story of a man meeting his long-lost brother on seeing a homeless man. Coincidences can happen.

Even an Old Sun Is Warm

This was inspired by:

• A trip to Loch Shiel and the Green Isle one summer. St. Finan resided on the island in the 7th century. Later it became a place for burials and a site of pilgrimage.

• Asking why science fiction is always about the extraordinary. Modern life would have seemed extraordinary a hundred years ago, but is very ordinary today, almost boring. Joseph and Louise had no interest in how they had travelled. It was an ordinary holiday for them.

On the Dot

- Solar flares are common and usually do not cause much, if any, disruption. Coronal mass ejections (CME) are less common and can be disruptive to all communications on earth and in space.

- Disruptive solar storms occurred in 2003 and 2005. Earth only escaped a very severe storm in 2012 because it just missed the planet.

- The sun activity fluctuates in 11-year cycles. The next active cycle will peak in 2024 and should be weaker than the previous cycle, but flares and storms can happen anytime.

- The UK's *Space Weather Preparedness Strategy v2.1* (London: Cabinet Office and Department for Business Innovation and Skills, 2015) uses the word 'resilience' 78 times.

- A Faraday cage will protect electronic equipment from magnetic storms such as CMEs. A simple metal cabinet is sufficient but any equipment must be insulated from the metal exterior. Cars are effectively Faraday cages and insulated from the ground by the rubber tyres, but damage to electronics can still occur and occupants are only safe if they are not touching anything metal.

• The author was one of those Cold War children who prepared for a nuclear war in the 70s and 80s. With a trunk packed they were ready to take the family from Dundee to the north west of Scotland. It felt very real back then.

Borrowed Time

• Jarrow in the north-east of England was a centre of learning in the 8th century. At the time it was called Gyrwe and pronounced 'yeerweh'. The abbey was next to the river Wear and was where the Venerable Bede wrote many texts including *The Ecclesiastical History of the English People*. In 734 Bede describes being too ill to visit Bishop Egbert in York who had been a scholar of Bede. However, he recovered and lived long enough to write a letter to Egbert and finish the last of his writings. He died on Easter day the following year.

• Fifteen thousand years ago sea levels were low enough to allow *Homo sapiens* to travel to many areas of the globe. Large grass savannas were home to antelope, bison and woolly mammoths.

- Motorcycle dispatch riders played an important role in WW1. The Triumph model H 500cc motorcycle was used by dispatch riders initially. It was notorious for stopping suddenly because its magneto got wet. Riders often used plasticine (invented in 1897) to seal the area around the high tension lead.

- The weather on the morning of Armistice Day was light rain and drizzle.
https://www.metoffice.gov.uk/research/library-and-archive/archive-hidden-treasures/end-of-world-war-one

- The pharaoh Akhenaten, father of Tutankhamun, built a new city called Amarna. It had been hurriedly built but 15 years later was abandoned soon after his death in 1332BC. Recent excavations have found tombs in which the bodies of mostly children, teenagers and young adults were laid. Many had injuries caused by hard manual work, suggesting child labour had been used to build the city.

- The Berlin Wall was built in 1961 to divide East and West Germany. Tunnels were one method used to cross and of those dug, one was ready on October 3, 1964 after 5 months of digging. Joachim Neumann had previously crossed to the West on a stolen Swiss passport and was determined to enable his girlfriend and family to escape. The tunnel was named because 57 people escaped to the West.

•   Leonardo da Vinci's preparatory drawing for the Adoration of the Magi from 1481 is one of his strangest. It contains the only camel and elephant he ever drew. It is an odd mix of people, rearing horses, walls and a trench, all in a building. Recent photographs taken in ultraviolet light have shown new features.* To the extreme right is a shape that could be mistaken for a tram (or even a Morris 1100). Leonardo left Florence for Milan soon after completing the drawing.

*See http://www.loc.gov/exhibits/leonardo/images/b-large.jpg

The Book that Sighed

• Entanglement of particles is part of quantum field theory and proposes that two particles can share a single physical state no matter how far apart they are.

• The films *2001 A Space Odyssey* and *I Robot* are different to the stories written by Arthur C. Clarke and Isaac Asimov, respectively.

• The lake scene with Mr Darcy in *Pride and Prejudice* was an invention of the TV writers and never appeared in the book.

• J.R. Tolkien smoked a pipe and in his *Lord of the Rings* the hobbits smoke 'pipe weed'. The culture of the 1960s and the later films hinted that more than nicotine was being smoked, but there is no evidence that Tolkein smoked anything other than tobacco.

The Books that Smiled

• Books destroyed and damaged during WW2 are listed in: Adrian S. Edwards (2013) Destroyed, Damaged and Replaced: The Legacy of World War II Bomb Damage in the King's Library. *Electronic British Library Journal*. Article 8, p.29 reports the loss of Ann Ford's 1778 book.

• 'Whiffle whaffle' was a term used in the 18th century to describe an indecisive time waster.

• Ann Thicknesse's book *Sketches of the lives and writings of the ladies of France*, was published in 1780. (printed for Dodsley, in Pall-Mall, London; and W. Brown, in the Strand).

- Ann Thicknesse (née Ford) played several stringed instruments and the glass harmonica well enough to play in concerts, much against her father's wishes. She spoke several languages, wrote and travelled widely. She was painted by Gainsborough in 1760. When travelling in France her husband died in 1792 and Ann was arrested and confined to a convent, being released two years later. She lived the last 18 years of her life with a friend, Sarah Cooper, dying at the age of 86.

- Margaret Clement (nee Gibbs) was raised by Sir Thomas More. She was the only one allowed to accompany Sir Thomas to his execution in 1535, and when he was granted a favour if he kept his scaffold remarks brief, he asked that his headless body be given to Margaret to bury. She risked her life to help the martyrs in Newgate Prison by smuggling in food. She managed this by virtue of her husband being the physician to King Henry, bribing the jailer and the fact she disguised herself as a milk maid. Eventually suspicions were raised and she was refused entry. The jailer allowed her to remove slates from the roof and lower food, but this too was stopped. Cromwell investigated Margaret's involvement but never proceeded against her and she escaped with her family to the Netherlands.

- The Gentleman's Magazine was published from 1731 to 1922 and was the first to use the term 'magazine'. Samuel Johnson was a contributor.

ACKNOWLEDGEMENTS

My thanks to family and friends, who were willing to read through early drafts and, despite that experience, still encouraged me to continue: Betty, Paul, Nina, Elizabeth, Margaret and Mike.

Nantia Koulidou brought her skills as a graphic designer to three of the illustrations. She was willing to listen to the foibles of the author without diverting from her designs.

Early advice was to find a professional proof reader and expert printer. Julie Musk (www.rovingpress.co.uk) was invaluable in conscientiously correcting my errors, especially my punctuation. The printer, David Exley (www.beamreachuk.co.uk) was patient with a new author and provided expert help.

My thanks go to St. Oswald's Hospice and Wirral Hospice St. John's who are partnering the promotion and sale of the book.

Finally, my thanks to patients, families and staff of hospices who inspired some of the stories.

Claud Regnard